KT-458-446

Gunpowder Empire

Raw hatred ravaged the range land!

Luke Bragg – a man with a dark past – has come to claim the sheep ranch his uncle left him. Only once he arrives in Preston Gulch, Bragg soon finds himself in the middle of a range war with the valley's two biggest cattle ranchers. This clash of interests, which Bragg tries to avoid, just escalates and he is the one the town thinks is the reason why. The cattlemen try to bolster their position by claiming that his sheep kill the grass by nibbling it too close and trampling the roots with their sharp hoofs. Then when the daughter of another rancher comes to town after the murder of her father, the truth about his death sends the valley into chaos and threatens the empires that they had established with gunpowder.

By the same author

Hell Paso
Shadow Peak

Gunpowder Empire

Matt Cole

A Black Horse Western

ROBERT HALE

© Matt Cole 2017
First published in Great Britain 2017

ISBN 978-0-7198-2397-8

The Crowood Press
The Stable Block
Crowood Lane
Ramsbury
Marlborough
Wiltshire SN8 2HR

www.bhwesterns.com

Robert Hale is an imprint
of The Crowood Press

The right of Matt Cole to be identified as
author of this work has been asserted by him
in accordance with the Copyright, Designs and
Patents Act 1988

All rights reserved. No part of this publication may be
reproduced or transmitted in any form or by any means,
electronic or mechanical, including photocopying, recording,
or any information storage and retrieval system, without
permission in writing from the publishers.

Typeset by
Derek Doyle & Associates, Shaw Heath
Printed and bound in Great Britain by
CPI Group (UK) Ltd, Croydon, CR0 4YY

October on the Sheep Range
By Arthur Chapman

There ain't no leaves to turn to gold –
There ain't a tree in sight –
In other ways the herder's told
October's come, all right.

Jest like ten thousand souls, all lost,
The wind howls – ain't it nice! –
The water-hole is froze acrost
With crinkly-crackly ice.

The sheep bed down before the sun
Has hit the rim of hills;
The prairie wolves are on the run
To make their nightly kills.

But kyards are sayin', 'Solitaire',
The bacon's fryin' prime;
The old sheep wagon's free from care
In late October time.

From *Cactus Center, 1921*

The Old Sheep Wagon
By Arthur Chapman

I have heard men long for a palace, but I want no
such abode,
For wealth is a source of trouble, and a jeweled
crown is a load;
I'll take my home in the open, with a mixture of
sun and rain –
Just give me my old sheep wagon, on the boundless
Wyoming plain.

With the calling sheep around me, and my collie's
head on my knees,
I float my cigarette smoke on the sage-scented
prairie breeze;
And at night, when the band is bedded, I creep,
like a tired child,
To my tarp, in the friendly wagon, alone on the
sheep range wild.

Music and art I am missing? – but what great sym-
phony
Can equal the harps of nature that are twanged by
the plains-wind free?
And where is the master of color to match, though
for years he tried,
The purples that veil yon mesa, at the hour of even-
tide?

I have had my fill of mankind, and my dog is my only friend,
So I'm waiting, here in the sagebrush, for the judgment
the Lord may send; They'll find me dead in my wagon, out here on the hilltops brown,
But I reckon I'll die as easy as I would in a bed in town!

From *Out where the West Begins, 1917*

CHAPTER 1

The wind had plummeted but the air was piercing enough to make Luke Bragg button his horsehide jacket at the throat as his horse plodded along the trail that skirted the spur. After his long trek along the long, prairie-flat preamble from the south east to where he was now, the land changed into two beautiful but distinct landscapes: the striated, fossil-rich sedimentary buttes of the Dakota badlands, and the nearby mountains so thick in evergreens that he had heard the native Lakota called them *paha sapa* – 'hills that are black'.

Not that the cold of the high range unduly bothered the big man. He sat loosely in the saddle, as if he had come a long way and was ready to go further. His horse was fresh enough; he had bought it back at Slocum, just north of the Dakota state line after leaving the Broughton stage. The horse was iron-shod; though the grade was steep, it was free of loose stone, and the long-legged gelding kept up a slow but steady pace.

When he reached the rim top, Bragg reined in and swung the horse about. There he stood by the graves of eleven men that were killed a few summers prior to his arrival – by the Lakota he could only assume. There was a sort of bulletin board about midway at the foot of the graves, stating the circumstances of the frightful tragedy. In short it said they were a party of fourteen, twelve men and two women, wives of two of the men. They had been camped on Plum Creek, a short distance from where the graves were. They were all at breakfast except one man who had gone to the creek for water; he hid in the brush, or there would have been twelve graves and no one to tell the tale of the massacre. Bragg could only guess what had happened to the women; he chose not to think about it however.

So he stared back the way he had come. It was surprising how high he had climbed; he could see the Cataract Valley spread out below, the river glinting like steel in the distance. The pile of ancient rock that made up the foothills of the Black Hills blocked his view of the upper valley, but he knew there was a town back there: Preston Gulch, not many miles distant.

It was, he reminded himself with a grim smirk, as he swung his horse to face the frowning saw-teeth of the higher range, a cattleman's town, and had been ever since the North Dakotas had been opened up.

The trail coiled around and down, and in a surprisingly short space of time Luke Bragg found himself descending into a shadow valley, like an oasis after the starkness of the hills above. A small river, which found its source in the higher range, passed right through the valley, to drop by a series of waterfalls and swift rushes to the Cataract below. The stream, fed by winter snows, had never failed to water the pastures of the valley.

Luke Bragg sent his horse forward at a quicker pace. The horse, seeming to sense his raised spirits, pricked its ears and needed little urging to move into an easy lope that brought it to the first gate. That gate was a surprise to Bragg, coming as it did like a mark of civilization in that solitary place. On either side of the stout gate ran a fence of meshed wire, and there was a line of barb on top. Again Bragg's lips tightened in that mordant grin. He worked his horse around, stooped from the saddle, opened the gate to pass through, and then closed the gate behind him. As he followed the trail across the first pasture he heard a foreign sound and turned harshly. Here was the reason for the meshed wire.

Sheep by the score, moving in that endless quest for food that seems aimless, yet is full of deadly purpose. He reined in his horse and, hands resting on his saddle horn, watched the grey-white blobs of wool moving across the grass.

Sheep!

Bragg knew only a little about raising sheep, but he had experience with cows. Cattle and sheep were simply turned loose in the spring after their young were born and allowed to roam with little supervision and no fences. They were then rounded up in the fall, with the mature animals driven to market and the breeding stock brought close to the ranch headquarters for greater protection in the winter.

And Luke Bragg reminded himself for the first time that Preston Gulch was in the heart of the big range, the old beef range.

Cattlemen's country! And from what he knew about cattlemen, they did not like sheep grazing on the open range.

He came upon his uncle's ranch house after receiving a letter a few years back where his uncle explained why he had chosen to raise sheep in cattle territory. The letter said, 'There seems to be no doubt that a vast quantity of mutton can be grown here, pound for pound, as cheap as beef; and, if so, then sheep-raising must be profitable as cattle-raising.'

He continued until he came upon the ranch without warning. The valley was lop-sided on a long slope and at the end of the floor was a towering stronghold of rock. The trail skirted it and there, round the other side, was the ranch house.

Bragg checked for a moment, staring at his inheritance, at the long, low ranch house with the barn close by and near it, horse corrals and the low fences of sheep enclosures. The place looked clean, well kept, but there was no sign of life, and from the galley chimney no smoke rose in the thin air.

He sent the horse forward again, stepped down near the horse corrals and tied his mount. He moved stiffly for a few paces, flexed his arms. The air seemed warmer in that pocket of land, the high rocks breaking the wind and holding the heat of the sun through the day. Bragg undid his jacket as he walked, and as the heavy garment fell back he dropped his hand to his gun and loosened it in its holster through sheer force of habit. When he was close to the door he called out, but no one shouted back a reply.

11

He climbed up to the door by way of the small stoop. He called out again without getting a reply. He put his hand to the latch; found the door opened easily enough. He thrust it back, walked in, sniffing. The air was musty, but there was a lingering smell of something – it might have been bacon cooked not long since. He wondered about his uncle's hired hands, but guessed they must inhabit the shack set a hundred yards back from the barn, close to the rock wall.

He strode into one room, found it empty, went out back, and retraced his steps. It certainly seemed as if the place had been unlived in since his uncle's death. But then again that was nearly three months back, he told himself, and went into the kitchen.

Again he noticed the smell of recent cooking on the air. He went to the stove. It had been put out, but the iron was warm.

He went out back once more, started to head round the side of the house towards the bunkhouse, changed his mind and headed back the other way, in the direction of the neglected patch of ground that might once have been a truck garden – raising their own crops to be consumed locally. Below it there was a chicken house.

He stopped short. There was a man right in front of him, his back to Bragg. The only remarkable thing about him, apart from the great shaggy sheepskin chaps wrapped round his legs, was the six gun he was holding. He was standing so still he might have been a cigar store Indian, Luke Bragg told himself. A grin quirking the corners of his mouth, he moved noiselessly behind the other man. Then he reached out, tapped the man on the shoulder and said, 'Lookin' for me, friend?'

The man in the sheepskin chaps went right on standing. He made no move to turn, and did not drop his gun. He went on staring past the angle of the house, and said in a muffled tone, 'I heard you, but I was too late to spot you before you got into the house. You must have switched and come around the other way. Sneaky. You must be one of Bonnadeen's men.'

'I'm not,' said Bragg. 'Never heard of the man.'

'That case, you must be from the sheriff's office. You are wasting your time, mister, I ain't going any place. You try to push me out and I will start blasting!'

'Maybe I have come to the wrong place,' Bragg supposed. 'This hell-raising outfit can't be the Black Hills.'

'Where else would it be?'

'Oscar Bragg's place?'

'The late Oscar Bragg,' countered the old man in sheepskin chaps. 'If you have come looking for him, feller, you are wasting your time – that is, unless you feel like clawing your way through six feet of hard clay to get to him!'

Luke Bragg stated, 'I don't believe in digging up dead men. And you had best drop that gun, friend.'

'Just say the word, mister, and I will wheel around and cut loose on you,' the old man replied sharply.

Bragg uttered, 'You sure are one hellraiser. I don't know who you were expecting, but I am glad I am not him. The name is Luke Bragg.'

The old man spun with an assurance.

'Merle Bragg's boy!' the old man exclaimed.

'Who else?' grinned Bragg, looking into the old man's

face. His first impression was of a long tangled beard that should have been white, but like the wool on the sheep out there in the pastures it had a filthy rain-washed look about it. Above the beard the eyes were emerald green, set deep below a tangle of brows that jutted over the cliffs.

'Merle Bragg's boy!' the old man burst out again.

'That is right. And who might you be, old timer?' Bragg inquired.

'Eckelmann. Only most times I get "Tramp". On account of what for most of my life I was a man without a home, I reckon.' He reached down and scratched behind one of the woollen leg coverings with the point of his gun, then, as if remembering he still held it, dropped it hastily into its holster, and extended an empty hand. 'I apologize for tryin' to bushwhack you that way, Luke. I am a peaceable man, but I sure meant it when I said I would shoot my way rather than get throwed off this place!'

As he shook hands, Luke Bragg said, 'I have heard tell of you. Before my old man died he told me about his brother Oscar switching from cattle to sheep, up here, and the trouble he had. Guess your reaction is warranted considering the trouble part.'

Tramp Eckelmann cracked up, his mouth opening to expose gums innocent of teeth. 'I guess I was born to trouble, Luke, and I will die that way! But see here, I thought you was never showing up.'

'You got the letter I wrote?'

'Sure,' nodded Tramp on the dot. 'It was just after the boys quit.'

'What boys?'

'Why, your Uncle Oscar's ranch hands. There was three

14

others besides myself – I have been the top hand around here – when your uncle's heart kind of gave out, and he keeled over, I held on. But the other boys, they reckoned they weren't going to have their scalps burned off by six shooters, not for any golden dollars. So they up and quit.'

'Leaving you and the sheep alone?'

'Why not?' Tramp shrugged indifferently. 'I have been looking out for myself ever since I was knee high to a day old lamb! Besides, I got an interest in this place.'

'How come?' Bragg asked.

'Your uncle deeded me a kind of share in some of the sheep he was running for wool. You will see it all writ down when you get the papers from those lawyer fellers.'

'All I have seen so far,' replied Bragg, 'is a copy of my uncle's will. There was mention there of assets covered in deed papers, lodged with a man named Sennett in Preston Gulch.'

'That would be key-rect,' nodded Tramp. 'Sennett was your uncle's attorney. He will take care of your inheritance. But, say, it is too durned cold to be jawing out here. Come on into the house, and I will get that stove going.'

He lumbered back indoors, unbuttoned his sheepskin jacket and strode over to the stove, where he busied himself right away.

'Guess I had better start at the beginning, Luke. But say, where did you say you came here from? Your uncle always spoke of you and your father, but never really said where you two were.'

'Originally from Ohio, after the war made our way to Texas, near San Antonio,' replied Bragg, and started looking around for coffee-making utensils.

15

Tramp stooped over the stove and said, 'By all accounts you never been up in this part of the country before?'

'That is right. I did most of my drifting, as I said, in and around Texas. A hell of a long way from these parts.'

'Well, what I was going to say was you maybe don't know it, but up in this part of the world there has been a whole heap of trouble between sheepmen and the others.'

'The others being cattlemen, I reckon.'

'Who else?' rumbled the old man, and paused in his talk to go out to the water cask. When he returned with fresh water he went on, 'Up around the Cataract the feuding's been worse than most places, on account of the sheepman got in these parts later than the cattlemen. They started up the other side of the Cataract Valley way out of Preston Gulch, and was running their flocks nice as you please, minding their own business, and not making any more trouble than a mouse in a haystack. Then the cattlemen started to get proddy over the use of wire and such. They moved in on the sheepmen. The cattlemen tried to strengthen their position by charging that sheep killed the grass by nibbling it too close and trampling the roots with their sharp hoofs. They pointed out that the odour which sheep left on the grass and in watering places was distasteful to horses and cattle. Of course, the sheepmen replied that, under good management, sheep and cattle could be grazed indefinitely on the same pastures, but cowmen were not convinced. The cattlemen then stated that the sheepmen were running their flocks too close to the high range, that side of the Cataract. The sheep men resisted – hot headed, hard headed, take your pick. Because they knew they didn't have the law behind them, they got mean and – well, you know how it goes, Luke.'

'I can guess,' replied Luke Bragg, taking off his jacket and tossing it over the back of a chair. 'There was a war.'

'There was,' Tramp acknowledged. 'How'd you know?'

'We had a similar conflict back in Texas a few years back,' Bragg said. 'In Brown County, Charles Hanna, who had brought the first sheep to that area just after the war, went out to his rock corral one morning and found that all three hundred of his flock had had their throats cut.'

'Our trouble did not start out right in the open – not for a long time. But it got that way the sheepmen didn't do a thing without looking sideways at the cattlemen first. You got to understand the cattlemen have got plenty of weight behind them around Preston Gulch.'

'Was force used against the sheepmen?'

'Boy howdy – indeed there was! Some was smoked out – and no questions asked. Others were scared most to death. One by one they got out,' Tramp replied.

'That was too bad; but how about my Uncle Oscar? He wasn't a sheepman.'

'Not until he seen that sheep was good business. All his life he had been a cattleman, same as your pa was, down there in Texas – where did you say that was called?'

'Big Tree, Texas.'

'Oh, yeah. Well, Oscar Bragg didn't give a damn about the silly notions cattlemen got about sheep. He talked to a lot of the sheepherders and he knowed they was onto something good. He said to me once, "Tramp, my heart ain't so good as it should be. Always helling around the high rocks chasing doggies, roundin' up the heavy steers

17

with a Norther blowing. I'm past it." So he went right out there and brought up seven or eight hundred head of woollies dirt cheap, on account of them scared herders pullin' out. Him and me, we moved them flocks clear across the Cataract and up into the Black Hills. We moved out in the open because Oscar Bragg feared no man, and reckoned he wasn't answerable to nobody outside of the Almighty. He sold off his beeves and his bulls, he hung up his branding irons, and he went bald headed for sheep. And it has been that way ever since,' Tramp retold.

'And trouble followed, I take it?' inquired Bragg.

'You take it, and you got it,' grinned Tramp Eckelmann, straightening at the stove. 'First, Hank Bonnadeen came to see him. Hank was an old friend of your uncle's, but he was chairman of the local Cattlemen's Association as well. He told Oscar he was a fool to keep sheep, that there would be trouble from the cattlemen this side of the range, that he had best quit his fool notions and get back to cattle.'

'And of course Oscar Bragg politely told him to go to hell, I bet?' Bragg said.

Again Tramp grinned. 'He wasn't too polite, but he was peaceable that time, compared with what happened when a full deputation from them cattle kings came riding in. It was around this time of day, I remember. There was five of 'em, and they rode right up to the door out there and me, I was having coffee right here with your uncle.' Tramp ran his blackened nails through his tangled beard and went on thoughtfully, 'Never seen a man move so fast as your uncle done that time. He grabbed up his scattergun from the wall, rushed out onto the porch, and aimed that gun right at Ben Flynn. It so happened Ben was the quietest of the whole bunch. He had only come along on account of that he felt he had to, I reckon.'

'Then what happened?' urged Bragg.

'Oscar Bragg yelled, "Ben Flynn, you take your friends and get the hell off my property! I give you to the count of ten. One, two, three . . ." He started to count just like that. Ben Flynn sat very quiet on his horse, saying not a word, though the scatter gun was aimed right at this head. Then one of the others, Rance Cash it was, from the Bar B, he up and yelled right back at your uncle, told him they was giving him one last chance to get rid of his flocks, or he would have plenty of trouble on his hands. So then your uncle again threatened to shoot and Flynn said something quiet to young Rance . . . they turned their horses around and rode out, like the devil hisself was after them.'

Bragg pointed out right then, 'Coffee's boiling.'

'Oh, yeah!' Tramp busied himself for a few moments then went on. 'Oscar Bragg wasn't a man to set down and wait for trouble to come to him. He talked things over with me that night, and first thing next morning, he harnessed up the rig, and drove right down to Preston Gulch. He went to the sheriff's office, and laid a complaint against the Cattlemen's Association – and remember he used to belong to that very same association himself!'

'Yeah,' said Bragg, 'how did the law take it?'

'Well, I will tell you this, Luke. We don't just have a sheriff down in Preston Gulch, we got Mick Gardner.' He paused impressively, but seeing no reaction on the tall young man's face, he snapped, 'Don't you ever heard nothing down in Texas? Mick Gardner's the man who cleaned out the Cannon Gang – they was around twenty or thirty hellraising cattle rustlers, owl hoots. They operated from the high range north of here, and they was so dug in nobody could reach 'em. The Cattlemen's Association offered a reward of a thousand dollars for the arrest of John Cannon, dead or alive. Six men went in to get him, and six never came out again. Then along came Mick Gardner, who was born and raised not fifty miles from here, give or take. He fought in the Indian wars and – well, he had one hell of a reputation. He rode right up to the hideout, and six weeks after he rode out again, and he was leadin' a horse and on it was a hogtied John Cannon hisself. He collected the thousand-dollar reward, and went back with a force of twenty or so men, backed by the cattlemen's bunch. They smoked out most every last outlaw from that hideout, and I tell you, boy, it was a right good day for the Dakotas!'

'Sound like he is quite the man,' said Bragg mildly, 'but how about my uncle and his troubles with the cattlemen?'

'Well, I'm a tellin' you about the kind of lawman we got. You see, after he cleaned out the Cannon bunch, and Preston Gulch being short of a lawman, he was elected to the office. I tell you there wasn't nobody voted against him, neither!'

'Good man, huh?'

'They don't come any better. What's more, he liked your Uncle Oscar. So there wasn't any doubt about your uncle getting' the backin' of the law in the feud,' Tramp replied.

'Now wait a bit. Mick Gardner didn't do anything to help the sheep men, did he? I mean the ones who were evicted?' Luke Bragg stated.

'Most of 'em had gone before he took office,' retorted Tramp. 'I ain't stretchin' it about Gardner – seems like you don't believe me! I'm telling you he ain't jest the fastest man with a six shooter, he's cold hearted, clear through!'

'All right,' said Bragg, 'you have made your point. So Oscar got the law behind him. So then what did he do?'

'Went right ahead and filed complaints, backed them with durned documents drawn up by Sennett, the lawyer, stormed into the Cattlemen's Association, braced Hank Bonnadeen hisself, had it right out with him then and there. I tell you, Preston Gulch was hummin' for a few days!'

Bragg was impressed. 'Then what?'

'Things kind of quietened down for a long spell. Hank Bonnadeen sided with your uncle, and Mick Gardner was ready to use his guns against anybody who harmed your uncle. The hotheads kept quiet,' Tramp continued.

'Who was the worst of 'em?' Bragg asked.

'The man I talked about before – Rance Cash.'

'Of the Box B, I'm guessin'.'

'Your guess would be key-rect,' nodded Tramp, and blew on his hot coffee. 'He inherited his old man's spread a year or so back, and I tell you, boy, he's a blacked-hearted hellraiser!'

'I take it the trouble didn't end there!'

'You are durned tootin' right it didn't! But when Oscar was alive he kept 'em kinda down. Everybody respected him and they knew he meant what he said and would stick by it right through. Then a few things happened, little things, but they kind of needled us, you know?'

21

Bragg looked puzzled. 'What kinds of things?'

'Well, for instance we got a little river runs through our valley. We call it the Whip. This Whip makes all the difference between a good ranch and a bad one. We depend on it – but so do a few cattlemen on the eastern side of the range. Somebody dammed it up one time, flooded our good pasture, and drowned a few ewes. And they poisoned off a few more, and for weeks the whole bunch of us patrolled that river, and we were not carrying our guns for show, neither! Things like that happened – shots in the dark – sheep found with their throats cut, cattle run through our wire, flattening it.' Tramp shrugged. 'Well, that was goin' on about the time your uncle up and died. Nothing big, but pinpricks that left sores.'

'How about this man you were expecting today?' Bragg asked.

'Hank Bonnadeen, from the Cattlemen's Association, served notice on me, as kind of caretaker for this spread, that I was to get out by the week's end. I figured that you must have been sent by him to see that I did.'

'Now my uncle's dead and the spread's changing hands, why do the cattlemen want to keep the feud going? Doesn't make sense.' Bragg began to pace a little.

'Does when I tell you that one week before your uncle cashed in his chips Ben Flynn died.'

'Flynn, one of the men who came here to talk my uncle out of raising sheep?'

'Yeah. The one Oscar threatened, held a gun on. Old Ben Flynn was plenty respected around here. So when his body was found, out there on his western line, with half his head blown off, there was a terrible scandal. He had been cut down in cold blood, and everybody said as how your uncle Oscar Bragg done it. If Oscar had not up and died hisself I reckon there would have been a lynchin'.'

CHAPTER 2

Mick Gardner came treading heavily down the wooden stairs that ran outside the frame law building where he lived in splendid bachelor isolation, to the sheriff's office below. Right alongside the office, in the back of which were cells, the courthouse stood, doing service most of the year as a community hall for dances and get-togethers, only functioning as a court when Judge Herman Allum showed up on his circuit.

There had been a sharp freeze the night before, and Gardner had his hands pushing into the fleece-lined jacket he was wearing, turned up to this ears. He was not very tall, but he walked as straight as a cavalryman, and a stranger, seeing the twin six shooters tied down on his lean thighs, would have known instinctively that the artillery wasn't there for show.

He walked briskly at an angle across the street to Marcus' Diner. From twenty paces away he could smell coffee and his nostrils twitched, and he yearned for the promise of warmth that awaited him from the coffee.

'Mick! Hold on there, would ya?'

Only one man in Preston Gulch used his first name like that. He checked and turned.

'Mornin', Tim,' Gardner replied.

A tall, thin man in his early thirties crossed the street to join him. Tim Sennett was a lawyer for whom a brilliant future had been forecast. But the bottle had beaten him and he would have gone all the way down had it not been for Ben Flynn of the Bar B Ranch – and his daughter Lena. They had made friends with Sennett and given him a good reason for living. Lena had also given him a good reason for staying on in Preston Gulch after he had quit thrashing around at sight of a bottle of rot-gut. She had steadfastly refused to marry him, but he never quit hoping. He was a good lawyer and the people of Preston Gulch trusted him. Even the warring cattle kings gave him grudging respect.

'Been waiting for you to show,' said the lawyer. 'Had breakfast yet?'

'Headed just now for the diner, Tim.'

'Then I will join you, I reckon.'

'Sure, come on along.'

They walked together into Marcus' place. Apart from few early flies droning against the window the diner was empty. As they took their seats at a table, the bead curtain was drawn back from the entrance to the kitchen and Marcus stuck his balding head out.

'Mornin', Sheriff, Mr Sennett. What's it going to be today?'

'Steak and eggs,' Mick Gardner shot back.

'Make mine just one egg,' Sennett said, 'and you don't have to fry it solid. Oh, and coffee,' the lawyer added.

As Marcus started to withdraw his head, Gardner called, 'Make it fast, Marcus! I have got a great hunger on me.'

'You most times have, Sheriff,' grumbled the hash slinger and disappeared. Sennett took out the makings and started to build a smoke.

'Oscar Bragg's nephew is here,' he said simply.

Gardner looked over at him with a mild eye.

'Maybe you didn't get it, Mick.' Tim Sennett kept it up. 'Luke Bragg, old man Bragg's kin, is here in Preston Gulch.'

'In town?'

The lawyer shook his head. 'He showed up at Black Hills yesterday. Old Tramp Eckelmann was in town last night. He had a few drinks at the Palace and then came to my office.'

'Liquored up?'

'No, he was sober enough. And it seems he did not do much talking in the saloon. But he told me about Luke Bragg showing up and how Luke intended filing his claim to the old man's land. It is all above board. Luke's the only heir and as far as the law's concerned, he can walk right in and claim Black Hills.'

'You figure he is going to make things tougher around here?' the sheriff queried.

'I don't rightly know, don't know much about this Luke Bragg. But by Tramp's reckoning he is all man. And mighty determined,' Sennett replied.

'To do what?'

'Stake his claim – and wipe the stain from his uncle's memory. Those are Tramp's own words, not mine, Mick.'

'I take it he knows all about the feud between the

sheepmen and the ranchers?'

'I reckon he does, sure. You can depend on it that old Tramp gave him all the details,' Sennett noted.

'Why didn't he come to the town himself?' asked Gardner.

'Tramp said he was taking a look around first.' Sennett paused. He could see the sheriff's brow was bent, and he was beginning to form a frown. 'Doesn't sound so good, huh?'

Mick Gardner made no reply for a moment. Then he fished a paper out of his pocket and before showing it to Sennett, said, 'Did you know anything about Luke Bragg before this?'

'I don't know about him now,' confessed the lawyer. 'Oscar never talked much about his kinfolk. Why do you ask?'

'Take a look,' replied the sheriff tersely, and handled over the paper. Sennett took one glance, then looked up startled.

'A telegram – and signed "Wade, US Marshal"!'

'Confidential,' nodded Gardner. 'That brief was telegraphed through just yesterday, from Poinsettia. Guess it speaks for itself.'

Tim Sennett read out slowly, 'Believe Luke Bragg headed your way. Could mean serious trouble. . . .'

'Hold it,' murmured Gardner. Marcus came bustling through the kitchen doorway with a tray full of viands. He proceeded to drop cutlery from a height of two feet onto the tabletop, then twirled a steaming platter in the sheriff's direction, juggled cups of coffee, slid Sennett's meal in front of him. Then he stood back in triumph.

'Eat that and live!' he pronounced.

'If I don't,' retorted Gardner, picking up his fork, 'I will come back and haunt you.'

Marcus went away laughing quietly, and Sennett said earnestly, 'Marcus can't hear us. What is all this about Luke Bragg?'

'You saw for yourself,' replied the sheriff, and put out his hand for the message. 'Bragg killed a man down there. The dead man was Drew Grigson and he was a known gambler.'

Sennett looked at the sheriff. 'That wasn't in the message.'

'I know all about it,' Sheriff Mick Gardner retorted. 'A check was made on all the north-western towns looking for a man they wanted as a witness. Bragg killed Grigson sure enough, but he was acquitted of the charge.'

'Meaning he wasn't found guilty of murder then,' replied the lawyer.

'Right,' nodded Gardner, attacking his breakfast. Between mouthfuls he went on, 'Seth Wade happens to be a friend of mine. He is marshal down at Poinsettia. He likes to keep me acquainted with things. Mighty useful at times, don't you reckon?'

Sennett blurted out, 'Well, what do you plan to do about this Luke Bragg?'

Mick Gardner calmly sawed off a piece of steak. 'What is there to do, Tim?'

'He is a wanted man!'

Gardner shook his head slowly. 'You are way off there, Tim,' he said. 'Bragg's wanted for nothing at the time.'

'But Marshal Wade telegraphed you—'

'And it was mighty unprudent of him – if there is such a word,' said the sheriff. 'I warned Cam Taplow to keep his mouth shut about this message, but I guess I can trust Cam just so far and no more. There has been so much talk about Oscar Bragg – and old man Flynn getting killed – that Cam might feel tempted to spread it around a little about Luke. I have got to take a chance on that but – I figured you might like to know.'

'I appreciate it,' said Tim Sennett, 'but surely this changes things a little?'

'How do you reckon?'

'Up till now,' said Sennett, 'I have been strictly on the side of law and order – and that means I was on the side of Oscar Bragg, too. I never gave a hang who won – the sheep men or the cattle ranchers. And, as you know, I didn't take sides over the Flynn killing, much as I wanted to.'

'I appreciate that,' said Gardner gravely. 'Knowing how close you were to Ben Flynn – and to Lena.'

'I like to be fair,' rejoined Sennett, 'and I always did like old man Bragg – touchy as he might have been at times. I never believed – and never will – that he had any hand in the cold-blooded shooting of Ben Flynn.'

'Me neither,' said the sheriff, mopping up the gravy on his plate. 'At the same time we can't close our eyes to facts, Tim. This valley's divided now. Most of the sheepherders have moved on, but the cattlemen are plumb determined to drive sheep out forever. They are using Ben Flynn's death as a lever, you might say, and now young Luke Bragg showing up might just spark off real trouble.'

'So I repeat – what do you intend to do?'

'Wait and see,' Mick Gardner answered back.

*

Luke Bragg rode with Tramp Eckelmann across the sheep lands of Black Hills, across the Whip and down through the open range, which Tramp said was all owned by the Flynn family.

'Sunrise is a fine spread,' sad the old man, as they rode along. 'Been in the family for years. Now I don't know what will happen. Ben Flynn left no heir – just the one gal, Lena.' The old man paused, but Bragg made no comment, so he went on again. 'Lena's a fine gal, don't get me wrong, but she ain't a man, now is she?'

'I will have to take your word for it,' laughed Bragg. 'But from what I hear, she is not a man.'

Tramp grunted, and stared fiercely about him, at last exclaiming, 'You know, this might be a crazy notion at that!'

Bragg looked puzzled. 'How come, Tramp?'

'We are on Sunshine range, and we are Braggs! Might easily get a bullet in the back of our heads at any moment.'

'We will have to take our chances on that. I want to see where Flynn was killed,' Bragg replied.

'I will show you, sure 'nough! But I am durned if I can see the point to it,' Tramp said begrudgingly.

Bragg made no answer and Tramp, grumbling to himself, kicked his horse into a faster run. Presently they came to the line fence, followed it for a time, and then as they entered a draw, Tramp checked his horse and said, 'This is about the place, give or take a few paces, I reckon.'

Luke Bragg reined in and looked about him. There was nothing remarkable about the place. The fence, which had run straight as an arrow for the past quarter mile, took a turn beyond the trees, mounted the hillside and disappeared from view. The grass, he noted, had been trampled by numerous hoofs.

'Who found him?' Bragg asked.

'One of his riders – Carver is one of the Sunshine crew. Old Ben Flynn took a lot of pride in his spread, and used to ride around it a whole lot. He was on his own that day – told his daughter somethin' about he wanted to meet someone at the line fence.'

'Did he say who it was?'

Tramp shook his head.

'Nobody knows who he aimed to see. He just didn't say. Seems Lena thought it funny he should ride off like that to meet up with someone and not tell her who it was. She sent one of his riders after him—'

Luke Bragg turned his head. 'Carver?'

'Yeah. He has been top hand at Sunshine since Clem Thayer took sick and went south to live with his daughter. Carver couldn't have been far behind the old man – least ways he was close enough to hear the shots,' Tramp explained.

'So he heard them, did he? That is interesting,' Bragg noted.

'So he reckons.' Tramp turned and spat deliberately. 'Me, I would take it with a grain of salt anythin' that Carver said – or did, for that matter.'

'What is wrong with Carver?' Bragg asked.

'Nothin' you can put a finger on, but I never did like the jasper somehow. Flynn was a good man and most times he had good riders on his payroll. But Carver, well, I dunno. Guess he is a good man with a rope and he sure is fast with a gun, and that is about all I can say in his favour.'

Luke Bragg had dismounted and was moving around. When he got closer to the fence he called back, 'Would that count with Sunshine? Carver being handy with a gun?'

Tramp shrugged, removed his hat and scratched his head. 'Wouldn't know about that. Mebbe on account of all the trouble there has been in the valley Flynn decided to hire him, Carver being a gunslinger hisself. He had only been on the Sunshine crew a few months when Flynn was killed.'

'Yet he was his top hand,' Bragg noted. 'That seems odd.'

'Reckon he got to kind of depend on Carver.'

'Because he was good with a gun?'

'Hell,' blew up the old timer, 'you do hammer away at a thing, don't you?'

Bragg gave a short laugh and climbed back in to the saddle of the horse.

'What are you after, anyways?' Tramp asked.

'Just wanted to know what it was all about,' replied Luke Bragg, and gathered up his reins. 'Now shall we head for town?'

Tramp grumbled quietly but loud enough for Bragg to hear. 'You sure like to get around too, don't you?'

Bragg cut the old man a sharp look. 'If you don't want to come, you can head right back to the house. No one is forcing you to tag along.'

'Now I didn't say that I didn't want to come along. . . .' Tramp began.

'After all, you were in town last night. And too much

liquor's bad for a man of your advanced age.'

Tramp flared, 'I don't have to be told when I have had 'nough licker, and when I ain't!' He added, as Bragg started to ride away, 'You had best wait for me! You will get yourself lost for sure!'

Luke did not answer but rode on, with a small grin on his face. He followed the fence. Tramp caught up with him in a moment, exclaiming, 'Seems to me you Braggs are a lot alike! You are just as mean as your uncle ever was!'

'Where is the break in this fence?' asked Bragg calmly, paying no attention to the old man's jab, as if he had not even spoken.

Tramp growled, 'Guess we will find a break about a mile or so up.' He added, 'We will have to cross the Bar B to get to the town trail. That is, 'less you want a ten-mile ride around.'

'We will take the short cut,' replied Luke Bragg. 'Who has the Bar B?'

'Rance Cash, like I told you. Cash is one of the big wheels in the Cattlemen's Association. Him and Hank Bonnadeen run together in most things. Of the two, I reckon Cash is the meanest. He is as hard as a barrel full of nails.'

Luke Bragg said nothing for a time, and then, 'Seems to me Oscar Bragg couldn't have picked a worse place to start raising sheep. With all these big ranches around and the cattlemen as tough as they come.'

Tramp nodded soberly. 'You are dead right there, son. But Oscar was as mule headed about sheep as he was about everything else he took up. When the other sheep-herders moved on, Oscar tucked his toes in and refused to budge. That was the way it went, and I guess it was just as well he cashed in his chips. Else he might have wound up like Ben Flynn with a bullet in his skull.'

Luke Bragg turned suddenly in his saddle.

'Tramp, who do you figured killed Ben Flynn?'

'You got me there, son. Guess there ain't no answer,' Tramp said with a sigh.

'But there must be! Figure it for yourself – if that store liquor hasn't already befuddled your mind too much!'

Tramp was hot under the collar. 'Now, see here—'

Bragg grimaced across at him. 'Keep those whiskers on. The way I see it, Ben Flynn was respected and a leader in the community.'

Tramp nodded his agreement. 'He was all of that, for sure.'

'He was running with the strong side, the cattlemen. From the way you have told it, I guess he was the strongest.'

'In size, sure,' Tramp said with another nod. 'Sunshine is the biggest around here. But Hank Bonnadeen and Rance Cash always were the meanest. Flynn was a mild kind of man, peaceable. He was the biggest loser when John Cannon was raidin' the cattle outfits, plunderin' and lootin' and rustlin' the cattle. But he never did holler as loud as Bonnadeen and Cash about his losses!'

'All right, then.' Bragg's tone was firm. 'The sheep-herders were moving out, and only Oscar Bragg was holding out against the cattlemen. It was just about a lone-hand affair.'

'Sure was! Like I told you, if your uncle hadn't been so well liked, he would have been smoked out the same as the others had been,' Tramp said.

'Then why the devil was Flynn killed?'

Tramp shrugged, removed his hat again and raced his hand through his graying hair. 'Search me.'

'But there must be some answer! Unless . . .'

He paused thoughtfully, and Tramp snapped, 'Well, what?'

'Unless the killing was done deliberately to throw the blame at my uncle,' Bragg answered.

'You mean—?'

'He had quarrelled with Flynn. He was the logical one to kill him,' reasoned Bragg.

Tramp shook his head. 'You are using fine jaw-breakers, young feller, but there is one thing that you have over-looked.'

Bragg narrowed his eyes as he looked at Tramp. 'What would that be?'

'There weren't no clear proof that Oscar Bragg, your uncle, done it. If they wanted to pin the blame on him, they would have left something around – like a hat mebbe, or an old boot, or—'

Bragg chuckled grimly. 'Or a calling card! But you are dead right, old timer. You have hit it right on the head.'

Tramp smiled, looking pleased. 'Glad I am some use, after all,' he snorted.

The two men rode on in thoughtful silence for a time, and then Bragg said, 'Throwing the blame on him might have been part of the reason. But the main part was surely someone wanted to get Ben Flynn out of the way – work off a grudge, maybe. Yet he had no enemies, you say?'

'None that I know of. He was a well-liked man,' Tramp

Eckelmann added.

'His killing might not have had anything to do with the cattlemen's feud – that is one thing to bear in mind, but. . . .' Bragg broke off, and to Tramp's surprise suddenly threw himself down on his horse's neck and at the same time went for his gun. Tramp jerked his horse to a standstill, and had opened his mouth to speak, when the unmistakable sound of a rifle bullet screaming overhead almost sent him tumbling from the saddle. By the time he had righted himself and started to feel outraged, Bragg was wheeling his horse off at an angle, still lying low in the saddle. But now his gun was out, shining in the sunlight.

'Back up!' The voice came from one of three men who had burst from the trees at the top of the rise.

'Cattlemen!' Tramp Eckelmann shouted.

The note in his voice checked Bragg, who slowly lowered his six gun as the three men rode closer. He saw that the man in the lead was tall, big built, black headed with a heavy black moustache like a bar across his upper lip. A few paces behind him rode a slim man, who sat tall in the saddle. The sunlight gleamed on a silver belt buckle and on the gay trappings of his horse. A few paces back and a little to one side rode a short, blocky man cradling a rifle in his arms.

'Back up,' said the man in front once more, then reined in. 'You Bragg?'

Bragg said nothing, and the gun was still in his right hand.

'This is Luke Bragg,' piped up Tramp, keeping both his hands in full view on his saddle horn. 'Kin to Oscar Bragg of Black Hills.'

'I didn't ask you.' The black-headed man still had his gaze intently on the younger man. 'What are you doin' on this range, Bragg?'

Still Bragg made no reply. He never did believe in wasting words, and right then he knew that danger was in the air.

'We was cuttin' through to the town trail, Cash,' said Tramp, not a bit abashed by the other man's rebuff. 'We came down through Sunshine and—'

'Carver.' It was the slim man talking. 'If this old Tramp goat does not quit gabbing, put a bullet through his hat.'

The old man's eyes snapped angrily, as the third man laughed. But he held his tongue while Cash edged his horse closer to Luke Bragg's and said, 'Things are touchy around here, Bragg. But I guess you know about that, don't you?'

Bragg eyed the stranger. 'I have heard some things.'

Rance Cash nodded briskly. 'You can put up that gun. We only sent that shot over your head as to warn you.'

'To warn me against what?' Bragg asked.

'To warn you that you two were trespassing, of course.'

'You own this range, mister?' Bragg asked.

'I am Rance Cash.'

'This the Bar B?'

Rance Cash nodded as he answered. 'It is! As far as your eye can see, this is my range.'

'You got a bar against strangers crossing your territory?' Bragg asked directly.

'Normally, no. This is friendly, open range, Bragg. But as you well know, there have been . . . difficulties around here,' Cash explained, then paused, but Luke Bragg said nothing – and still made no attempt to holster his gun. 'This gent here is Hank Bonnadeen. He owns the next spread, the Crazy 8. He feels like I do that strangers are not welcome on the open range right now.'

'If I had known that,' said Bragg politely, 'I would have taken the long way around.' He pitched his voice a little higher. 'Not that I am blaming you, Tramp. I guess you only wanted to please.'

Tramp, surprised, opened his mouth to speak, then shut it again. He had already formed the opinion that Luke had the Bragg wits, all right. He wasn't talking just for the hell of hearing himself speak.

The next moment Bragg said, 'When we go to town tomorrow or the next day, Tramp, we will be sure to take the long way round. Remember that.'

Rance Cash said, 'There is a clear trail into town from Black Hills. Not that you will be staying here long, Bragg.'

Bragg showed very little in his reaction and then said, 'I figure I am staying as long as I want.'

'We won't argue over that,' said Cash. 'But just bear in mind that we are a mite quick on the trigger around here these days.'

'I will remember it,' Bragg added, then in the same tone went on, 'I guess that gunfighter of yours back there had best remember that the next time he looses a shot over my head he is liable to get one right back – only mine will be cast low.'

There was a shocked silence for a moment, then Tramp grinned broadly.

Luke Bragg said, 'You got my message, Carver?'

Carver, his swarthy face dark with anger, suddenly

heeled his horse forward and slung the rifle into firing position over his horse's head.

'If you don't drop that six gun within five seconds flat, mister, you are going to be dead!'

Bragg drawled, 'You got a warrant for loosing that thing off on the open range?'

'He needs no warrant,' said Cash sharply. His tone had changed, and the muscles on his jaw were standing out like cords. 'This is Bar B country, Mr Bragg.'

'And Carver rides for you these days, I take it,' Bragg noted.

'It seems you are well informed,' said Hank Bonnadeen in his silky voice. He moved his horse on ahead a little so that all three now were ranged in line, facing Luke Bragg. 'Carver does ride for the Sunshine people, but he is also employed by the Cattlemen's Association, of who I have the honour to be the chairman.' He paused impressively, but Luke Bragg showed not a flicker of interest. 'So you see, my friend, Carver is on his home range in any part of this valley. You might call him one of our watchdogs.'

'Glad to have that cleared up,' said Bragg amiably, 'but I will go on record as saying I don't like being shot at – by watchdogs or anybody for that matter.'

He saw Carver jerk his head towards Bonnadeen and mutter something swiftly. But then Rance Cash stepped in. He snapped, 'It looks like we had best get this cleared up once and for all, Bragg.'

'Get what cleared up?' Bragg asked.

'This business of you being here,' Rance Cash articulated clearly.

'Do I have to spell it out for you? We are not trespassing

– only taking a short cut through to the trail.'

'I didn't mean that! And I refuse to talk to you unless you put up your gun,' the rancher put into words.

'Talk to your watchdog first, Mr Cash,' Bragg shot back verbally.

Again the muscles stood out on Cash's cheekbones, but he turned sharply and said something to Seth Carver who, with an ill-natured look on his face, slowly lowered his rifle, then dropped it into its saddle sheath.

'Your turn, Bragg!'

'Why not?' Luke Bragg tossed the gun in his hand, then holstered it. He saw the almost imperceptible look of relief that passed over Cash's face.

Hank Bonnadeen was silent but Cash said, 'That is much better! Now then – why have you come to this country?'

'Oscar Bragg was my father's brother,' he replied.

'I am aware of that fact. Did he deed you the ranch?' Cash inquired.

'He did – if it is any of your business.'

Hank Bonnadeen said smoothly, 'Anything that happens around here these days is our business, Bragg.'

'I will remind you that I am not in your line at all, Bonnadeen. I am taking over sheep country!'

Cash leaned forward in the saddle. He said angrily, 'You a sheepman, Bragg?'

'I can be anything I have to be. Just name it.'

'To save peace in this valley, my best name for you would be one-time owner of Black Hills!'

Bragg shot the man a stern look. 'Meaning?'

'I will be quite frank with you, Bragg. We don't want

sheep farmers around here.'

'Guess there is plenty of range for all.'

'That would be where you are wrong. Dead wrong, Bragg!' Cash said angrily.

Hank Bonnadeen raised a hand. 'Allow me, Rance. Bragg, it may be hard for you to understand. You are an outsider – I don't know anything about you, or where you are from, but by the looks of you, you have punched cattle in your time.' His eyes flickered over Bragg's rugged frame, taking in the smooth, scarred chaps, the good but worn boots, the horsehide jacket. 'Cows, Bragg?'

'I have done my share of punching,' Bragg replied.

'You say this is a big range. It is, but it is a limited range. We are hemmed in by hills – mountains, if you like! There is plenty of water, plenty of rivers, but the country is fenced by nature, and that means we have nothing up here like the wide pampas, the big grasslands to the south.'

'And so?' Bragg deliberately kept his tone polite.

'We have our problems as cattlemen, Bragg. For years now we have been trying to solve them. Then came the sheepherders. To keep those woolly critters in they had to put up fences – that was to be expected. The fences went up, and then wire to keep the cattle out – and the mountain lions as well, and the marauders that threatened the sheep. Where we had one problem before, the sheep men gave us a dozen more.'

Rance Cash said angrily, 'We don't have to give you the whole story, Bragg! Anyone with any sense can see that this is cattle range, always has been, and always must be!'

'All very well, far as it goes,' said Bragg, 'but I guess the sheepman has as much right to make a living as the next man.'

'We are not denying that,' said Hank Bonnadeen quickly, before Cash could retort. 'But the sheepherders would not play along. They would not help us solve those problems, would not cooperate.'

Bragg cocked his head slightly as he responded, 'That isn't the way I heard how things went!'

'I don't know how you heard it, Bragg, and right now I am not all that interested. The truth is, most of the sheep-herders came to their senses in time and moved on to better pastures – better sheep country! Sheep have no business eating the grass meant for our steers! But your Uncle Oscar was stubborn and thought differently. He held out. Well – he up and died, and that is the end of that as far as we are concerned. Now you come along, say you are claiming the inheritance and going to move in. We would like to tell you here and now that you are wasting your time.'

Luke Bragg flashed a slight grin. 'I seldom do that, Bonnadeen.'

Rance Cash said, 'The weight is against you, Bragg! Come to your senses, boy – and come to them quick!'

Bragg shot the rancher a harsh look. 'You threatening me, Cash?'

'Not yet! I only hope it does not come to that,' Cash answered.

'Then what would you call it, Cash?'

Cash leaned forward in the saddle. 'Want to bargain? I will make you an offer here and now – a good offer – a Cash offer,' he smiled at the pun, 'an offer for Black Hills.'

Bragg turned his head to the side. 'This is a genuine offer, Cash?'

'That is Mr Cash to you,' snapped the rancher. 'We could always use a part of Black Hills. It is good range – good cattle country, as Oscar Bragg proved over many years! Why in the hell the old fool had to go and turn to those fool sheep I will never know. . . .'

'All right, Rance.' It was Bonnadeen again, with his silky voice. 'The past is best left buried. My advice to you, Bragg, is not to let it bury you, too.'

Bragg was getting real tired of the threats. 'Threats again – veiled threats, Bonnadeen?'

'Take it any way you please, Mr Bragg. My advice to you is to take Cash's offer.'

'Is it from him, from the Bar B, or from the Cattlemen's Association?' Bragg demanded of the ranchers.

'We have to have a meeting about it,' Bonnadeen said.

But Rance Cash was growing impatient. 'Are you willing to sell, Bragg? Here and now, sell out, and get the hell out?'

'No,' said Luke Bragg. 'I am not willing to sell. I am staying on.'

Now they stared at him with hatred in their eyes. Now he knew for the first time that these were no ordinary ranchers; they were big men used to having their own way, fighting the smaller men, fighting the sheepmen through cussedness or greed or just the desire to prove how strong they were. Then he knew how real the war must have been – and how real it was then, at that moment, with the sun high in a frosty blue sky, the grass green beneath his horse's hoofs.

Hank Bonnadeen whispered, 'Turn your horse about Bragg. And start riding.'

Luke Bragg said, 'One word, gentlemen.'

'We will hear no more from you,' snarled Rance Cash. 'You heard what Hank said. Ride out!'

Bragg's eyes flashed anger. 'And if I don't?'

'You will be dead! Dead as that old mule uncle of yours, Oscar Bragg!'

Carver's thick voice joined in. 'Good thing the old mule died or he would have swung high for what he did to Ben Flynn.'

To the watchful eyes of Tramp, Luke Bragg suddenly seemed to sit taller in the saddle. He rapped out, 'You are a liar!'

Instinctively the two ranchers swung their horses clear, leaving Carver in the centre with only a few yards between him and Luke Bragg.

And Seth Carver cursed cheerfully and went like lightning for his gun.

For an agonizing second, the old timer Tramp prayed that a thunderbolt might fall between the two men. Not for nothing had the Cattlemen's Association privately paid Carver to ride for them. He had the name, the weight, the reputation. And now the gun was in his hand.

Bragg seemed to draw slowly – a dragging, limping movement. And yet, as if by a miracle, his was the first shot plunging across the narrow space. And even as he fired, he pitched himself sideways in the saddle, leaning far out and heeling his horse so that it leapt the other way, and now his arm was curling over, the sights coming down to take the second shot.

But no second shot was warranted.

Carver, the darling of the cattlemen, the crack gun, was rearing from his saddle, his arms thrown wide, gun spewing from his fingers. He cried out something not understandable, then tumbled headlong to the ground. With a convulsive leap, his horse started forward, and the body was dragged for a few yards, then cast off like so much jetsam, to sprawl in the grass.

'Take it up, gentlemen – draw your guns. Take them up or get out of my line of fire!' roared Luke Bragg.

The two ranchers, aghast, stared back at him. They saw a new Luke Bragg, whose face had darkened somehow, as if by an inward fire, whole body tensed now that he was upright again in the saddle, his gun barrel tilted skyward, with the forefinger tight about the trigger, ready to bring it into instant action.

'Your choice, gentlemen! Make it fast or you will be joining your hired gun!'

From the side, Tramp Eckelmann croaked, 'Take it easy, son. Take it easy.'

Cash responded, 'The law of this territory . . . prevents trespassing on occupied ranges near settlements, but away from the settlements . . . as we are now . . . the shotgun or pistol is the only law, and sheep and cattlemen are engagd in constant warfare, Mr Bragg.'

To him the sign of the killer was written large in the sky. The ranchers saw it too. White faced, Hank Bonnadeen forcibly turned his horse about, and sent it at a frantic run up the hillside. For an instant Rance Cash hung back. His mouth was gaping below the black moustache, then, as Luke Bragg slowly lowered the shining gun barrel towards him, he, too swung his horse about and raced after Bonnadeen.

'We will get on to town now, I reckon,' said Luke Bragg calmly. 'Time's awastin'.'

CHAPTER 3

Sheriff Mick Gardner saw the two men as they rode into the town of Preston Gulch. He was standing on the porch of the law office as they went past, and watched them as they rode on down Main Street and tied up their horses outside Tim Sennett's office.

So Luke Bragg was going to make his takeover of Black Hills legal, the sheriff told himself grimly. With sudden decision, he jerked his hat over his brows, walked to where his horse was tied. Swinging into the saddle, he glanced back to the rack where the newcomers had tied their horses. Now he had seen Luke Bragg, he had the feeling that whatever he might have done down south, he looked well able to look after himself in Preston Gulch.

He made his way to the telegraph depot, where he found Cam Taplow at his key. The sheriff waited until Cam had finished taking a message, then, leaning over the counter, said, 'You busy there, Taplow?'

'I am always busy, Sheriff!' The telegraph operator glared up at him from under his eyeshade. 'Reckon I would be the workingest man around this town – bar none!'

'Any more messages come through for me?' Gardner asked.

'Heck, no! Wasn't expectin' one, was you, Sheriff?' Cam said.

'You never know in my job,' replied Mick Gardner. 'But, say now, Cam, meant to remind you. Keep it quiet about that message I got from the marshal of Jackson Springs.'

'The one about Luke Bragg?' said Cam Taplow.

'That is the one, I wouldn't want that news spread around town, if you get me. . . .'

Cam Taplow said violently, 'I told you at the time I wouldn't say nothin'! I ain't no gabber, Sheriff!'

The sheriff nodded in response then said, 'That's all right, then. Just thought I would remind you, that's all.'

'I don't need no remindin'! You do your job, Sheriff, and I will do mine,' Taplow fired back.

'All right, all right,' grinned Mick Gardner. 'No need to get in a lather over it.'

He was turning away when Taplow said, 'Say, Sheriff, you seen Bragg yet?'

'He has been around,' the sheriff answered back.

'What kind of lookin' jasper is he?'

'Just a man like you or me, Cam,' Sheriff Gardner said calmly.

Taplow said indignantly, 'I ain't got any likeness to a wanted killer!'

Mick Gardner's expression changed. He said sternly, 'You've got it wrong there. Luke Bragg was cleared of that killing. He is not wanted for anything . . . presently.'

Cam Taplow looked unconvinced. 'Seems durned funny to me. This Bragg must have been a hellraiser down Jackson Springs way – and – if he was in Jackson Springs pen, he might have met up with John Cannon!'

Gardner frowned suddenly. Strangely, the thought had not hit him before. Now, mention of John Cannon brought back recollections and disquieting thoughts as well. He said in a flat tone, 'Jackson Springs's a big jail!'

'I reckon it is, it would have to be awful big to keep a man like John Cannon lost!' Cam chuckled. 'Reckon Cannon was lucky at that. He got away with a killin' but John Cannon is in Jackson Springs for keeps – guess they will bury him there.'

'Yeah, I suppose,' said the sheriff, and tapped impatiently with his fingers on the counter top. His thoughts were busy as Cam rattled on.

'Me, I will never forget that day when you brung John Cannon in. Reckon it was the biggest day in Preston Gulch's history!'

'It is all over and done with now,' said Mick Gardner absently.

'It won't be forgotten though,' said Taplow confidently. 'Ain't every town gets an outlaw big as Cannon brung in – and then has the man who caught him for sheriff!'

Without smiling, Gardner said, 'You will have me blushing next.'

Cam Taplow cackled. 'Bit of a change for you, Sheriff, noseyin' around this quiet town, nailin' drunks and wastin' my time. Don't you ever wish you had another John Cannon holed up in the hills?'

'I never want another,' replied Mick Gardner quickly

and quietly. 'They have got him snugged down there at Jackson Springs and it would take an earthquake to bust him out!'

Taplow seemed annoyed by his confidence. 'Too bad you didn't get the backing you needed at that time, Sheriff,' he said maliciously, 'else you would have had every man jack of Cannon's bunch behind bars.'

'We got the men we wanted.'

Mick Gardner shook his head. 'But not all of them! Brother-in-law of mine over at Gainesville was talkin' with me the other day. He reckons some of Cannon's bunch got together again when the heat cooled down. There is talk of tryin' to get Cannon out of Jackson Springs, so they can all ride the owl hoot again.'

Mick Gardner smiled faintly. 'No hope of that, Cam. Sorry to disappoint you, and your brother-in-law! They will never get John Cannon out of Jackson Springs! But – I can take a hint. I won't waste any more of your valuable time. But don't forget what I told you about Luke Brag. Keep it quiet – you hear?'

Cam Taplow snorted. 'You don't have to tell me a hundred times over! I ain't some dang fool! But, come to think of it, this Luke Bragg might be just what the town needs – a little gingerin' up.'

Sheriff Gardner went out into the sunshine, thoughtful now, remembering John Cannon and the ugly scares when singlehanded he went into the hills to get him. Surely it was only coincidence that Luke Bragg should have been in this Jackson Springs pen where they were holding Cannon – the biggest prisoner the state had ever held. Hell. After all, it was natural that Luke Bragg should come to Preston

Gulch to claim his inheritance. There was nothing sinister about it.

And yet as Mick Gardner rode back into the heart of town his thoughts were heavy, and when he got to his office it seemed that all of his fears had been justified. Lena Flynn was waiting for him.

Lena Flynn would have been a striking woman even on the busy streets of New York, Chicago, or San Francisco. She was tall, as her father had been, and she had a mane of dark red hair that she wore piled high, giving her extra stature if that were needed. Her skin was pale, her eyes beneath the dark brows warm and lustrous. Lena was a serious-minded girl, who had been close to her father. His violent death had shocked her immeasurably. At once she had dropped her plans to go east for the winter, and set about with great resolution to take over the ranch.

When Mick Gardner walked into his office the girl rose to her feet and faced him. He saw that her eyes were dark with anger; her mouth, usually quick to smile, downturned.

'I have been waiting for you, Sheriff,' she said impatiently.

'This is a pleasant surprise, Miss Lena! Won't you sit down?' He gestured awkwardly to the chair she had vacated but she nodded her head.

'I came in just as soon as I heard the news. One of my hands – my top hand, fact, Seth Carver, has been murdered!' she said emphatically.

The sheriff frowned. 'Murdered?' he echoed.

Lena nodded briskly. 'And I know who killed him, too.

It was Luke Bragg. Does that name mean anything to you?'

The sheriff took his time replying. After staring at her for a few moments, he moved carefully around to the other side of his desk, stood there staring at nothing. Presently he said, 'You had best tell me about it, Miss Lena. Tell me everything you know.'

All this time Luke Bragg had been in Tim Sennett's office with old Tramp sitting in the background fidgeting, for he had little patience with legal talk. Sennett, for his part, felt uncomfortable throughout. Knowing what he did about Luke Bragg, he found it difficult to dissemble. Yet if he hadn't known anything about Luke Bragg's past he would have found it hard not to like him. As it was, he felt nervous, ill at ease, even while he explained the documents that he held in relation to the Black Hills ranch. Luke Bragg was quiet throughout, and all the questions he asked were intelligent ones.

At the end, when the deeds had been signed, Sennett said, 'Does this mean you intend to settle here, Mr Bragg?'

Without hesitation, Luke Bragg replied, 'Sure.'

'Well, the place is all yours!' Sennett fidgeted with papers for a moment and then said, 'Do you realize that you might get opposition from the local ranchers? Even trouble?'

'Yeah!' exclaimed Tramp from his chair. 'We seen some of that opposition already!'

'In that case—'

Bragg spoke up. 'Don't waste time trying to talk me out of this deed, Mr Sennett. Here I am and here I aim to stay.' He got to his feet, reached for his hat. 'Bill me for the

52

work you have done on this. Once I get things straightened out I will be banking here in Preston Gulch and you can keep an eye on that side of affairs for me as well.'

'Happy to do so,' mumbled Tim Sennett, not meeting Luke's gaze. He knew that Luke had his hand outstretched, and at last forced himself to get to his feet and shake hands. 'I hope you . . . you settle down all right.' It was all he could manage to say.

'Be seeing you around,' said Tramp, and followed Luke out through the doorway. As he closed the door behind them, he said, 'Well, I don't know how much Sennett's goin' to bill you, but I reckon them lawyers oughta pay a man to sit and suffer all their jawing. Say now—'

'Hold it,' said Luke Bragg quietly. He had seen the figure standing back on the porch, the wink of the badge. 'You want something, Sheriff?'

'I am waiting for you,' said Mick Gardner. 'That is, if you are Luke Bragg?'

With a puzzled look on his face, Bragg shot back, 'That would be me.'

Tramp said eagerly, 'Luke, this is Mick Gardner I told you of. He is the man that brought in John Cannon—'

'All right,' said the sheriff, moving in, hand on gun butt. 'Tramp – I mean Rufus, you had best come along with us. Your name has come up too.'

'Come up about what?' the old timer fired back.

'The killing of Seth Carver. Better give me your gun,' the sheriff pressed for.

'You plan on holding me for that shooting?' Bragg inquired.

'What I plan on is talking to you about that shooting,'

the sheriff replied.

'Then you won't be needing my gun.'

'Best play it my way,' said Gardner, without raising his voice. 'I am thinking you are smart enough not to make trouble, Bragg.'

Luke Bragg stared into the sheriff's eyes, then slowly he drew his gun, reversed it, and handed it over without incident.

Tramp said indignantly, 'He killed Carver fair and square, Sheriff! I was there and I seen it meself—'

The sheriff did not react to the old timer's words. 'We will just go down to my office,' he said thrusting Bragg's gun into his waist belt. 'The quicker we get there, the quicker we get it over with, gents.'

'This,' said Sheriff Mick Gardner, 'is Lena Flynn.'

They faced each other: the woman stood tall and proud, a hit of curiosity in her eyes, yet still a lurking shadow of anger; Luke Bragg, big and powerful, his face as inscrutable as an Indian's. Against her will she felt the compulsion of his gaze, the power that radiated from him. She heard herself saying, 'How do you do?' And the next moment flushing as she remembered who he was and what he had done.

'I am pleased to meet up with you, ma'am.' His tone was gravely polite.

Hat in hand, he faced her, and from the side Sheriff Mick Gardner said quietly, 'We had best clear this up once and for all. Bragg, Miss Flynn's brought in news that her top ranch hand has been killed. Her information is that you did it. I want to know what you have to say, Bragg.'

'It won't take many words to tell you, Sheriff.' Luke Bragg still had his eyes on the woman. 'But, before I start, I want you to know that Carver was riding, not for Miss Flynn at the time, but for the Cattlemen's Association.'

Lena exclaimed angrily, 'That has nothing to do with it! He was my rider, on my payroll!'

Sheriff Gardner said gravely, 'Just give us the facts, Bragg.'

From near the door, Tramp said, 'Carver was killed when them cattle ranchers forced a showdown! He went for his gun, and Luke here went for his'n and—'

'All right,' said the sheriff sharply. 'We will leave Bragg do the talking! What did happen out there?'

Luke Bragg told him, as simply as he could. The telling did not take very long. When he was through, Lena Flynn turned restively away, sat quickly on a chair, stared at the floor. Mick Gardner, standing like a statue by his desk, said at the end of it, 'That seems clear enough. We won't go into the whys and wherefores of it now.' He turned to Tramp. 'I take it you'

'Durned right I do.' Tramp turned to Lena Flynn. 'I can see you are feelin' a mite proddy about this, Miss Lena, but I am tellin' you that Carver never was no good! He was a murderin' polecat and today he showed his hand!'

'That will do!' snapped Sheriff Gardner, before Lena could speak. 'The point is that you and Bragg have given your side of the affair, and I guess Miss Lena's had another—'

'I heard an entirely different version!' The woman had her head thrown back and was staring with hostility at the silent Luke Bragg. 'The way I heard it, you and Tramp

55

were crossing Bar B country when you met Bonnadeen and Cash, Carver was with them—'

'I will say he was!' exclaimed Tramp. 'He was totin' a rifle, too! Like Luke said, he let loose a shot over our heads—'

'Will you be quiet!' The woman was on her feet. 'I am told that Bragg was warned off the range, told he was trespassing. He then turned ugly, went for his gun, and Carver tried to defend himself, but was too late. Luke Bragg shot him dead.'

'Well, that is a durned lie,' shrilled Tramp, his eyes flashing but the sheriff strode over to him and grabbed him, not gently, by the shoulder.

'One more squawk out of you, old timer, and I will put you in a cell!' snapped the sheriff.

'I have a right to stand up for my friends, ain't I, Sheriff?' demanded the old timer, not a bit abashed.

'You can stand up for who you like, so long as you stop talkin' once in a while!' The sheriff turned to Bragg. 'It looks like it is your word against theirs, Carver can't give us his version of the incident, can he?'

'Two against two,' nodded Bragg, 'but, being a fair minded man, I can see that the odds are against me.'

'How come?'

'The other two are local men and big ranchers, I am an unknown, and I guess you can't take old Tramp's word, as he worked for my uncle and now works for me,' Bragg reasoned.

The sheriff shook his head. 'That has nothing to do with it, Bragg.'

'Then you don't agree that the odds are against me?'

Bragg asked.

Sheriff Mick Gardner said evenly, 'I am not the judge and jury, Bragg. I am only here to keep law and order in Preston Gulch.'

'And to see that justice is done,' flared the woman. Her hands were clenched at her sides. 'Carver was on my payroll and I am demanding that you do justice here and now, Sheriff!'

'Now take it easy, Miss Lena. . . .'

The woman was adamant. 'I demand that you arrest this man, and have him tried for the murder of Seth Carver! If you refuse. . . .'

'I shall telegraph to Jackson Springs for the US Marshal! I am determined not to let this matter rest or take it lightly, Miss Lena,' the sheriff responded.

The three men stared at her, and even Tramp was silent for once.

Then Luke Bragg said in his quietest voice,

'I am quite willing to stand trial, even in a town dominated by these cattle ranchers.'

Tramp exclaimed, 'You gone loco, Bragg! They would have you hung before you could sneeze!'

Bragg said to the sheriff, 'If this is a hanging matter, then I will stand trial for it. I have got the crazy, old fashioned notion that an innocent man doesn't have anything to fear.'

Sheriff Mick Gardner stared back at him. He said, 'The old frontier laws have gone, Bragg. Once a man could shoot another and not be answerable to any jury, just so long as he didn't shoot his man in the back. But now – this is a peaceable county. Miss Lena's entitled to demand justice for the death of one of her men.'

'I appreciate that,' replied Luke Bragg curtly. 'Why wrap it up in a lot of words? I have already told you that I will step right into one of your cells, and wait for the trial judge – just as long as you can guarantee that I will come to trial!'

'There will never be a lynchin' in this town while I wear this badge,' snapped Gardner. 'I didn't aim to apologize for Miss Lena's demand! I just wanted to make clear to you how things are done around here.'

'You didn't have to tell me. I have been around a long time, Sheriff. And Preston Gulch isn't the only town with good law in it,' Bragg stated.

'I am glad to hear that!' the sheriff replied.

'Right,' said Luke Bragg. 'At the same time, you're trying to tell me that you never had any gun play in your fine little town?'

'We do have it, at times,' responded Gardner.

'Drunken brawls,' snapped Lena Flynn. 'Squabbles between cowpunchers and—'

'And worse!' exclaimed Tramp. 'Why pretty it up, folks? Till Mick here took the badge, Preston Gulch was as hellin' a town as you had meet up with in the north! And even now we get our trouble – like when that sheepherder was set fire in his hayrick!'

Lena Flynn took an angry step forward, but Gardner kept his lips closed, almost as if for the first time he wanted Rufus to go on talking.

'You denyin' that, Sheriff? You, Miss Lena?' Tramp gave an angry laugh. 'Durned right you ain't, for the reason it is true, and you know it! Ever since sheep was brung into this territory there's been trouble – shootin's and poisonin' the water, and men bein' run off their homesteads like they was nothin'!'

'That is all very well, old timer,' Lena said, 'but cold blooded murder is a different thing—'

'Different, is it? You oughta be the last one to squawk about this bein' a peaceable town – seein' as your own father was cut down by an unknown—'

'Some people believe that my father's killer had a name!' The girl spoke hotly, without thinking. 'My poor father's dead body is calling out for vengeance—'

'And justice, Miss Lena?'

At the sound of Luke Bragg's voice, the girl was jerked into silence. She turned slowly to face his quiet eyes. He said, 'I heard all about that killing, Miss Lena. I have also heard that my uncle was suspected of it. One of the reasons I aim to stay on here is to clear his name.'

The girl exclaimed, 'And isn't it just possible that you wasted no time in getting even with your uncle's enemies? Carver wasn't just my rider – he was used by the Cattlemen's Association – and now he is dead . . . dead by one of your bullets, Mr Bragg!'

'Take it easy,' Sheriff Gardner had moved between them, his hands upraised. 'This is getting us no place fast. Miss Lena, your father's death has nothing to do with this.'

'How can you prove that?'

'I am not trying to prove anything. I want to get to the bottom of Carver's shooting, and I will. In the meantime, I don't aim to hold Bragg on the say so of those ranchers,' Carver said.

'Yippee!' Tramp snatched off his hat and waved it.

'You can't do this!' Lena Flynn, all fire, faced the sheriff squarely. 'You can't just turn him loose!'

'I said I wasn't holding him, Miss Lena. It is his word against theirs and—'

'And you refuse to take the word of two reputable men? Men who have been in this country for years,' Lena Flynn snapped.

'If Carver was killed fair and square, I am not holding Bragg.' Gardner's tone was suddenly sharp. 'You are forgetting that Rufus Eckelmann has been around just as long as anybody else. He may be a grabby old fool—'

'Thanks, Sheriff, for them kind words,' Tramp said with a grin.

'But I have never found him out in a lie!' When Lena was silent, Sheriff Gardner went on, 'Sometimes we get a mixed-up idea of what actually happened. When things have cooled down a little, I will get a clearer story out of the ranchers and I will take a look at the scene itself, it might have something to tell me, I suspect.'

'I doubt it,' Luke Bragg shot back. 'By this time, I guess, they will have taken away Carver's body, but I can tell you now that he didn't have time to fire his gun – his six gun, that is. Like I told you, he fired a warning rifle shot over our heads from the cover of the trees. From that position, by the way, they must have seen clearly who we were, and it is my hunch they wanted to scare us off.'

'You say they offered to buy Black Hills from you?'

Bragg nodded. 'They did.'

'I will back that up, too, Miss,' Tramp put in. 'Cash played it all nice and quiet till Luke refused to sell, said he was stayin' on. It was then he showed his mean streak.'

'All right, old timer.' Gardner shrugged his gun belt into a more comfortable position. 'I am accepting all that, for now. But the rest I am leaving open.'

'Then I am free to go?' Bragg asked.

'Not too far,' warned the sheriff. 'I have got no han-kerin' to go chasing all over the north west for you – you hear?'

'You won't have to chase me, Sheriff,' replied Luke Bragg quietly. 'Any time you want me I will be out at Black Hills.'

'Just how long do you think we will let you stay there?' demanded Lena Flynn, and Bragg turned on her swiftly.

'You linking yourself with Cash and Bonnadeen in this war against the sheepmen, Miss Flynn?'

The colour rose darkly in her face. She stammered. 'I am – I am a cattleman – I am taking over from my dead father.'

'Against me, Miss Flynn?'

'Against anyone who wants to break the peace—'

'And if I don't break the peace? What then, Miss Flynn? You aim to take the war into Black Hills?' Luke Bragg snapped.

'Take it easy, Bragg,' murmured Sheriff Mick Gardner, but the woman flared.

'If you want war, you will get it,' Lena Flynn answered sharply.

Luke Bragg did not back down. 'Looks like I will get it simply by staying on my own land with the likes of you and other cattle ranchers.'

Lena said, 'I tell you, it is cattle country up here!'

'It is also a free country, ma'am, and if I want to raise

sheep or rear goats, Miss Flynn, I will do as I please!' Luke Bragg was firm and adamant.

Tramp cackled from the side.

Lena said, 'My father died because of this war, Bragg! Now another good man is dead—'

'Are you putting Seth Carver in the same class as your father?' Bragg asked, astonished.

Lena cried, 'Of course I'm not! I—' She broke off and whirled on the sheriff. 'I am not going to stand here and trade words with this – this drifter! I have already told you what I intend to do – and I am going to do it, Sheriff!'

'You aim to call in the US Marshal from Preston Gulch, Miss Lena?' asked Gardner gravely. 'If you do, give him my kindest regards. He is an old friend of mine.'

'Why, you – oh, all you men stick together!' Head high, she swept out through the doorway.

Luke Bragg said, 'Bitterness goes deep in this town, Sheriff.'

'Don't make it any deeper,' said Sheriff Gardner, and their eyes locked.

CHAPTER 4

The next few days were extremely quiet; in town folks went about their business, and out on the big cattle spreads work went ahead on winter preparations, for there were cattle to be moved, fences to be checked and repaired, beeves to be cut out and trailed southward to catch the late markets before the freeze set in.

Besides Black Hills, there was only one spread remaining in the valley that ran sheep in any quantity. This was the old McPhail homestead, taken over by Wilson Cameron, who, with his son Jack, had worked hard in the past couple of years to build up a sizable sheep herd from pastures set narrowly among the foothills east of the Whip. Cameron had been one of the last to feel the weight of the cattlemen's displeasure. Largely because of his isolation he had been left more or less alone until the time came when his supplies were cut off from the town's main store, and a bunch of ewes vanished one night through a gap in the wire – a gap that had been made with cutting pliers. Wilson Cameron and his wife were quiet folks, hailing from Kansas. They were hard working and believed in peace at any price. Without showing any anger against the things that were happening to him, Cameron ran off the main flock of his sheep, sold at the best price he could get, and turned to raising root crops in the shadow of the great hills. He still had a few sheep, but now the cattlemen worried him no longer. The Association made it plain to him that unless he kept well clear of the cattle ranges he would have to leave as so many other sheepmen had done in the past six months. Wilson Cameron went on with his homesteading a quiet man, not easily fazed.

On a trip to town he heard about the coming of Luke Bragg, and the shooting of Seth Carver on the Bar B range. He also brought back to his wife and son the news that Sheriff Mick Gardner had decided not to take any action against Bragg; that Carver had been killed in a fair gun fight, and for the sake of peace and quiet in the valley there would be no official move to force Bragg to leave.

The following morning Luke Bragg was riding across the high country above the ranch house, which was now his own. Tramp was working a bunch of sheep further down the valley, towards new sheds that the two had built the day before in readiness for the approaching winter.

Luke Bragg saw the horse and rider coming in over the rim. He shook his gun loose in its holster, and waited. When the newcomer was within hailing distance, he checked his horse and raised his right hand, palm outward, as an Indian would have.

'I am Wilson Cameron. I want to talk,' he said.

Luke Bragg eased his horse towards the man, who, he could see as he drew nearer, was craggy, in his middle fifties, a sun-weathered man with sunken eyes and a chin beard.

'You must be Luke Bragg,' Cameron added.

'That is right, Cameron,' Bragg replied.

'I have McPhail's old place a ways east of here. Maybe Tramp told you about me?'

Luke Bragg nodded. The past few days he had heard details on just about every resident in the valley, for Tramp certainly loved to talk.

'I am told you were a sheepman once.'

'Still am at heart.' Cameron's deep-set eyes were taking in the big young man who sat loosely in the saddle. 'Is it true you aim to stay on here?'

'They will have to carry me out,' Bragg said in response.

'Maybe they will try to do just that,' Cameron fired back.

'Guess you know all about that, Cameron?' Bragg said.

'I could have fought them,' replied the homesteader frankly, 'but I have got kinfolk – my wife is nervous. Almost an invalid, you see.'

Bragg stared back at the man. 'So you didn't fight?'

'None of us did, mister – outside of old Oscar Bragg. Too bad he up and died . . . he was stubborn enough to take on all of them pesky cattlemen.'

'You admired my uncle?' asked Bragg.

'Couldn't help admirin' him. Mind, he was wrong-headed about a lot of things. You see, the small man – a homesteader like myself – he can't fight a bunch of men like Cash and Bonnadeen. They are too big. Just too big, and that is the truth of it.'

'You own your land?' Bragg asked.

'By frontier law, I own it. I got just as much right and title to it as Flynn of Sunrise had,' responded Cameron.

'Did you have a grudge against Ben Flynn?'

Wilson Cameron's lined face showed no resentment as he shook his head briefly.

'I don't hold no grudges, not even against the men who cut my wire and let my sheep through to lose themselves and drown themselves all in the middle of the night. No, mister, I always had a lot of respect for Ben Flynn, and I sure was sorry he got killed in that fashion. Matter of fact, the Sunrise line runs clear across my bottoms. I had a lot to thank Ben Flynn for – he often did me a kindness and so did that daughter of his,' Cameron stated.

'What did you come by for today, Mr Cameron? Curious to see what I looked like, perhaps?' Bragg questioned.

For the first time a smile showed up on Wilson Cameron's thin lips. 'Guess everybody's a mite curious about you, Bragg. A whole lot of wild stories are being circulated about these parts, I found out last night when I was in town gettin' supplies. But I wanted to find out first hand, you know, for myself whether you was goin' to stay on here or not.'

Luke Bragg remained still and said calmly, 'I am staying.'

'Mind tellin' me what your plans are, Bragg?' Cameron probed.

'I aim to run the spread – run it the same as my uncle did – and if I can make out half as well as he did, I will be satisfied.'

Wilson Cameron nodded. 'Sheep or cattle?'

Luke Bragg gave a short laugh. 'Which side are you on,

Mr Cameron?'

'I don't take sides, mister,' Cameron fired back.

'And just what does that mean?' Bragg asked intently.

'Like I told you, I am a peaceable man. I have got a sickly wife and young son I am trying to raise the best way I can. Range wars are not for me. I don't ask for much from anyone and I don't quarrel with my neighbours,' Cameron responded bluntly.

'Being neutral, how do you stand right now?' asked Bragg.

'Just where I have always stood, I reckon. I mind my own business and expect others to do the same as me.'

'Seems to me the cattlemen are not playing by your rules, Mr Cameron,' noted Luke Bragg.

'Just as long as I can make a living out of my homestead, I will be content,' Cameron said simply.

'Then you figure the big ranchers will let you go on that way?' Bragg asked.

'Just as long as I don't run sheep all over the range,' Cameron relented.

Luke Bragg stared back. 'That mean you will quit for good then, Mr Cameron?'

'That's right, Bragg. That is what I wanted to see you about. But first up, I wanted to know just what you figgered on doing around here,' Cameron remarked.

'I take it you are not asking just for the hell of it then, Cameron,' noted Bragg.

'You are right there, Bragg. I ain't drawing cards either way. What you do is your own business.'

Luke Bragg again nodded before responding, 'Then why ask me about it at all?'

'I still have a few sheep, Bragg.'

'What of it?'

'I want to get rid of them. While I have them around they might be a temptation to some of them trigger-happy cattlemen. You want to buy them off of me?' asked Wilson Cameron.

'How many have you got?'

'Around a hundred head,' Cameron answered quickly.

Luke Bragg nodded slowly. 'Guess I could take them off your hands, if the price was right.'

'I could meet you there,' replied Cameron. 'They are in good shape – around half of them are full-grown ewes, the rest are younger stuff with a couple of rams thrown in.'

'I better come over and take a look at them, I reckon.'

'You are welcome any time. But say, you don't look like a sheepherder to me,' Cameron noted.

'Is that so?' Bragg shot back.

'Cattle, yes, but somehow I can't see you pushin' around a flock of woolly critters,' Cameron almost laughed.

'We will see how it goes,' replied Bragg noncommittally.

'Guess we will.' Wilson Cameron stared thoughtfully into the middle distance for a time, and then, 'You got a stubborn streak in you, same as your Uncle Oscar had?'

Bragg shrugged slightly. 'Maybe so.'

'Reckon must be something like that. Well, sheep or cattle, all comes to the same thing just so long as you can sell them and make a few dollars. Me, I like to sleep peacefully at nights, and not have worries whether or not my hayricks are going to be there when I wake up in the morning. Reckon it takes all kinds . . .' Cameron paused.

'When you figger on comin' over?'

'Right away, if it suits you,' Bragg said directly.

'You like them, you aim to driver them off?'

'Sure, don't see why not,' answered Bragg.

'You will need help. Them sheep ain't like cattle. They need driving. . . .'

'I will take your word for it. I haven't had much to do with the woolly critters. The way I heard it, you start one walking and the rest follow along . . . like they are witless or something,' Bragg said.

'Ain't as easy as it sounds. One makes a break and the others follow, sure enough. And once you have started them walkin', they will walk along mild enough. But you got to keep them in a bunch, and you need dogs for that,' Cameron elaborated.

Luke Bragg hung his head. 'Dogs, huh?'

'Yep,' nodded Wilson Cameron. 'And seeing as I am going right out of the sheep business – and ain't goin' to keep myself even mutton raisers for my own table – I will let you have a good dog I trained myself. He is from the real sheep country, east of here, the other side of the big range. He knows his work, and he will save you long hours in sweat and bad temper.'

'That is mighty neighbourly of you, Mr Cameron, but I reckon you had best put a price on him with the rest of our flock,' Bragg suggested.

Wilson Cameron smiled. 'Gladly . . . and I am obliged.'

Together they swung their horses about and set off for the river.

CHAPTER 5

At the same time when Luke Bragg was over at Wilson Cameron's place closing the deal over Cameron's sheep, Lena Flynn was at the Bar B with Hank Bonnadeen. A mood of burning indignation had stayed with Lena, ever since her run-in with Luke Bragg. She felt she had to talk things over with someone, and naturally she thought of Bonnadeen, who, she knew, had been one of her father's associates. Not that she knew any of the ranchers or their families very well. Lena had spent most of her adult life away from Preston Gulch, had had a good education back in the east and had spent a lot of time travelling. But she had always come home to Sunrise, for the links between her and her father had been very strong indeed. She had been in a restless frame of mind at the time of his death. The tragedy resolved things for her. She made up her mind that she would stay on at Sunrise, and keep it going as her father would have wished her to do.

Lena Flynn was a wealthy woman, for Sunrise had been prosperous for many years. But she had always been lonely. Her mother had died when Lena was just a young girl, and she had few close friends in the valley. At Sunrise she relied upon the housekeeper, Mrs Singer, to run the big ranch house for her. She employed eight regular riders on the spread, together with others at times when extra help was needed, at round-up and such. Seth Carver had been made top hand before Ben Flynn had made up his mind about the man, largely by virtue of his undoubted skill and by the strong backing he had had from the Cattlemen's Association.

Ben Flynn had naturally been a member of the Cattlemen's Association ever since it had been founded. He was the biggest rancher in that country and his word carried a lot of weight. A different man would have used that weight to his advantage; Flynn could have easily dominated the Association, and for that matter called the tune throughout the whole valley. But he was a quiet, retiring sort of man, with no real wish for personal glory.

During the running war with the sheepmen in the valley Flynn had stood to one side, refusing to go along with the threats and violence used by the other cattlemen. His death removed the only moderate member of the Association. The big men were all like Bonnadeen and Cash; the smaller ones did not count.

Bonnadeen was not surprised to find Lena Flynn in a tearing rage about Luke Bragg. Bonnadeen had already had news of the release of Bragg from the sheriff's custody – like all small towns Preston Gulch had its own system of rapid communication; news could spread faster than by telegraph at times.

'Don't worry,' he told the woman, 'we will make Bragg pay for killing Carver.'

'I don't want any more bloodshed—' Lena cried.

'Did I say there was going to be any?' Bonnadeen surveyed her blandly, hands thrust deep into the pockets of the heavy hunting jacket he wore. Somehow he gave the woman confidence, although there was something about Hank Bonnadeen she vaguely disliked; almost as if he was too suave, too sure of himself.

'I hope you are right,' she told him doubtfully. 'I thought of getting in touch with the marshal at Jackson Springs, but Sheriff Gardner told me that the marshal happens to be a great friend of his. So what would be the point?'

'That would not solve a thing,' replied Bonnadeen, with decision. 'Legally, you could file an indictment for murder against Bragg, but we are back where we started from – he has a witness and so have we. It is our word against that of that old fool Tramp.'

Lena said earnestly, 'Mr Bonnadeen, you did tell the truth about what happened out there, didn't you?'

He surveyed her blandly, his eyebrows raised in mock surprise. 'Miss Flynn, why should I lie about a thing like that?'

'It seems strange that Gardner should take a stranger's side like that of Bragg,' she reasoned.

'Against us? There is nothing strange about that. You haven't lived as long as I have – nor seen as many towns just like Preston Gulch. I never yet met up with a sheriff who was eager to jail a man for shooting another man in an open fight,' Bonnadeen said firmly.

'But you said Carver had no chance!'

'Well, maybe I stretched that a little—' he almost smiled

in his response but caught himself.

'Stretched it! Did Seth Carver go for his gun or didn't he?' Lena demanded to know.

'Now, take it easy, Miss Flynn.' For the first time there was a trace of acidity in Bonnadeen's voice. 'Don't put me in the witness box, if you please! What I told the sheriff was the truth. Bragg cut Carver down in cold blood.'

'But if Carver went for his gun – if it was a fair fight. . . .'

'You know nothing about these sort of things,' he said sharply. 'There is a difference between a gunfight and what Bragg did to Carver. You can take my word for that, Miss Flynn.'

'For the first time I am starting to wonder just what did happen out there,' Lena said without hesitation.

'What difference does that make?'

She stared back in utter disbelief. 'It makes a lot of difference to me, Mr Bonnadeen!'

The rancher's eyes narrowed. He said nothing for a moment, then, 'Just what does that mean?'

'Carver was nothing to me. As a person, I mean. When I first heard of the way he had died, naturally I wanted to see justice done – his murderer brought to trial! But I refuse to whip up any indignation in his favour, just because he was my top hand and a first-class man with a rope!'

'You are suddenly losing your desire for justice, Miss Flynn,' Bonnadeen said.

She flushed, then exclaimed, 'Of course I stand by justice! But though I am younger than you, Mr Bonnadeen, and certainly have not been around as much, I do know that men fight on the open range with guns – it is the law of this country. The unwritten law. And until we reach a higher stage of civilization it will always be that way!'

Bonnadeen was not amused. 'So now you are convinced that Seth Carver died in a fair fight, is that what you are saying, Miss Flynn?'

'I am merely saying,' she said sensing the man's anger beginning to rise, 'That I am having some doubts.'

'Then there is nothing more to be said,' Bonnadeen snapped.

As he started to turn away, Lena said quickly, 'Listen to me, please! I am anxious as you are to have things back to normal around here, in this town and in the valley. . . .'

'Normal? You mean with sheepherders horning in on our cattle range? With foul waterholes, and barbed wire?' Bonnadeen was starting to lose control of his contempt.

'You know perfectly well that isn't what I mean! More than anything I want to do away with all this feuding and bloodshed! At the same time, I am not going to stand by while men like Luke Bragg walk around as if they were free to kill anyone, anytime they want and get away with it!' explained Lena Flynn.

'Now you are making more sense,' Bonnadeen said with a half smile. 'Trouble is, Miss Flynn, like most women, you want the best of both worlds! Don't forget that your father died – just like Carver did.'

'It wasn't the same thing at all! Let's be fair about it, Mr Bonnadeen.'

'Fair?' Again his eyes narrowed. 'I don't know the meaning of the word, Miss Flynn, when it comes to dealing with sheepherders! That goes for Luke Bragg, too. He isn't getting away with this or anything, I assure you of that.'

She paused to calm herself. 'What do you propose to do?'

'You came out here to get my advice on that, did you not?'

'Yes, I confess I did, but—'

'Don't start changing your mind. That is my advice to you, Miss Flynn. What's more, leave men's work to the men – believe you me, Rance Cash and I can handle this! And in the wind-up you will be on the winning side.'

Jack Cameron had just turned nineteen and was proud of the fact that he was a grown man now. He was also happy to be riding away from the narrow confined acres of this father's spread. Luke Bragg had bought the sheep, ridden with Jack and his father behind the hurrying flock down the pasture and up the steep slope on the other side. His father had told Jack to keep the flock moving, with the help of the dog, Prince, whilst he and Bragg made their way round the spur of the mountain to steer the sheep through the narrow and difficult divide when they emerged in the open. At that point, the trail swung treacherously round the mountain before reaching the top of the valley, where the Black Hills pasture lay.

Jack Cameron found the going easy enough until he reached a point some halfway along the divide. Here, the mountain wall rose steeply at this left hand, whilst the trail running narrowly traversed the naked spur, with a drop of a hundred feet or more down the other side. Jack whistled to the dog, which instantly ran along the flank of the pattering bunch of sheep, funneling them into a narrow phalanx. Jack eased his horse back so that he would not crowd the woolly critters in the rear, and so hasten their pace. Prince, big and shaggy, ran backwards and forwards, tongue lolling, thrusting a glance every now and then at the precipice below. Jack gave him one whistle and brought him back. There was no danger, he knew well. Just a little caution and they would be through the narrow place, pass down the rest of the divide, and so break out into open country and the safe pastures beyond.

Suddenly the sheep in the lead checked, skittered one way and then another. They were obviously scared by something. Angrily, Jack rose in his stirrups as he checked his horse with a violent hand. For a moment he could not see what had caused the panic. Then the hard winter sunlight struck on gun metal, and he saw a man sitting a horse up the trail. He was partly obscured by a jutting rock, and at first Jack thought he was a stranger. Then, as the horse moved into full view, he recognized the man and shouted, 'Murdoch! Murdoch, get the hell out of there!'

The man who had been watching the panic-stricken sheep turned his head, and Jack could see the grin on his face. Clint Murdoch was a Bar B rider, and Jack knew him well.

'Can't you hear me, you loco fool? You are scarin' the sheep!' Jack called out.

As if Murdoch hadn't heard him, he moved his horse forward a few paces, thus completing the panic in the sheep closest to him. They were jumping on each other's backs, milling together in a grey-white tide. Jack knew that it only needed one foolish critter to make a frantic dash too far to the side, and he would lose the whole flock over the edge of the precipice. With a surge of fury, he drove his horse forward yelling, 'Damn you, Murdoch! Get off the trail!'

He fumbled for the old Sharps rifle he carried on his saddle. As he broke it clear, he turned his head swiftly to see what had happened to the dog. Prince was for the moment out of sight, but the next moment he broke clear, scampering along the edge of the drop, silently, purposefully working the sheep back.

'Get them back, boy!'

For a moment it seemed as if the dog would do just that. But just as the bunch started to swing away from the edge, Clint Murdoch, up the trail, swooped forward, raising his arms and yelling. Appalled, Jack Cameron hauled in his reins, dragging his horse to a standstill. Before he could give a shout or do anything, one of the leaders of the flock ran clear over the edge, to be followed in a matter of seconds later by the sheep on its heels. Then the rest started to go over in ones and twos, and in little baa-ing bunches – like the Gadarene swine, they went headlong over the cliff.

Then Jack Cameron, a red haze before his eyes, was thundering along the shelf, heedlessly scattering the few remaining sheep running hither and thither as if uncertain where to go. Among them, despairingly, ran Prince, barking furiously.

'Too bad about your sheep,' laughed Murdoch.

And then he saw the rifle coming up to Jack's shoulder as he rode. Swiftly he dived for his gun. But before either could shoot, a rifle exploded from the defile out of which Murdoch had emerged. The bullet sang briefly and Jack

Cameron, struck in the chest, was hurled backwards from the saddle, his rifle flying from his hands to smash on the rocks at the lip of the gorge. He hit the ground and rolled, then lay still. Murdoch swiftly turned his head and laughed, calling out, 'Good shootin', Dan! But I could have stopped him myself.'

The second man moved out into the open. Dan Waters, tall and black bearded, one of Rance Cash's riders from the Box C. He didn't laugh with Murdoch. Instead, he looked across at where young Jack Cameron lay and snarled, 'That goes for all sheepherders!'

'How about the rest of this bunch?'

'We will roll them over with the rest,' Waters fired back.

But, before either man could move, a faint shout came down the defile. 'Hello there, Jack!'

Swiftly the two exchanged glances. Then Waters said, 'Old man Cameron and the other one have worked their way around. Let's get outta here!'

Clint Murdoch, no hero at the best of times, was already heeling his horse at a fast run down the trail. Dan Waters followed, and as Cameron's dog ran snarling at his horse's heels, he swore at the animal, jerked up his rifle as if to use it again. He failed to see that young Jack had rolled over, and was attempting to get to his knees. Ashen faced, he stared after the two fleeing riders.

And then, with a clatter of hoofs on rock, Luke Bragg and Wilson Cameron came into view. For an instant they checked their mounts, staring as if in disbelief at the shrunken flock huddled beneath the rock wall – and at young Jack, who had collapsed again, the blood pouring from him.

Luke Bragg was the first off his horse and at the boy's side. As he raised him up, Jack mumbled, 'Dan Waters – he done it. . . .'

Bragg said urgently, 'Take it easy now, son! What happened here?'

'Murdoch – he run the bunch over the edge. I went for him – Waters bushwhacked me . . . Pa, I'm sorry. . . .'

Wilson Cameron was standing over them, making no attempt to get closer to his son. His face was hard as the stark rocks about him. He said, in an odd, lost voice, 'You done well, Jack. You always done well.'

'Pa . . .' said the boy again, and then settled against Luke Bragg's encircling arm.

For a moment Bragg stared down at him, then looked up and said quietly, 'I guess he's gone, Mr Cameron.'

He gently eased the boy back on the rock, got to his feet, his mouth a hard line. He looked into Wilson Cameron's eyes and saw such a cold fury as he had never seen in any man before.

'Waters,' Luke Bragg said. 'Waters and who was the other one?'

'Clint Murdoch,' mouthed Wilson Cameron. 'Murdoch, of the Box C, and Waters of the Bar B. You want to make war on them cattlemen, Bragg, you just got yourself a recruit! All right, what are we waitin' for?'

CHAPTER 6

The tracks were hard to follow. But Waters and Murdoch had to stick to the trail, at least until they reached the open country at the foot of the narrow valley in which Wilson Cameron's ranch was situated. Luke Bragg, with Cameron tagging grimly behind, sent his horse fast down the trail while it was confined by the mountain. Then, when the country opened up, he reined in and turned to Cameron with a question in his eyes.

'They wouldn't swing right,' said Wilson Cameron. 'They must have gone that way.' His finger pointed to the direction he referred to. 'That way lies the Sunrise spread. They would have to cut through the bottoms there.'

'And then?'

Cameron shrugged, his eyes bleak and tinged with redness.

'Your guess is as good as mine, Bragg.'

'I will take a look,' said Bragg. Taking the lead, he zigzagged down, his eyes keenly scanning the ground. At last he picked up the tracks he had been searching for – rock, newly scarred, the print of half a hoof on a minute patch of soft ground. He sent his horse on more quickly now, and presently Cameron ranged alongside him.

'Reckon they would head up for higher country?' Wilson said.

Bragg shot him a look and asked, 'Which way?'

Cameron nodded his head towards a belt of scrubby trees jutting from outcrops of rocks away to the right. 'The other way they would have to cut wire to get through Sunrise. They can't be far ahead of us, but they will be pushing their horses mighty hard, I reckon.'

Without a word, Luke Bragg sent his horse forward. He made no attempt to search for tracks until he was within striking range of the trees. Then he cast about, and to his satisfaction found fresh prints. He took time out to turn in his saddle, and to nod to Cameron, who clutched his rifle to his chest with his left hand, his right hand bunched about the reins.

So they rode on, climbing now, and presently they were into the trees, through them, their horses grunting as they breasted the steep slope.

'Swing to the left,' said Wilson Cameron unexpectedly.

Bragg, without hesitation, pressed his horse around.

They rode in silence for a few minutes and then, 'Got a hunch,' whispered Cameron tersely, and Bragg gave a brief nod.

Soon they were on the rim top and they checked their horses. Cameron, sitting like a graven image in the saddle, stared slowly about him. Suddenly his voice cracked out, 'There they go!'

Below the rim the ground fell away into bad grazing country on the borders of the Box C. There were grey-green rocks and a few stunted trees, and at the bottom of the slope a sluggishly flowing creek. Bragg squinted in the hard sunlight, then focused on two figures, minute at that range, climbing the slope beyond the creek.

'It might be them,' he said, but Cameron was already surging his horse forward and Bragg, with a shrug, followed him. They rode openly down the slope until Bragg turned with a warning and said, 'Best circle around!'

Wilson Cameron didn't seem to hear him, but went plunging on. Luke Bragg worked his horse closer, barking out, 'We have to circle, Mr Cameron! Play it my way, you hear me?'

Cameron turned bleak eyes, hesitated for a moment, then nodded. The two horses, flecked now with spume, their saddle leathers slippery with sweat, went obediently around the rocks, descended to the creek, splashed through and grunted up the other side. Luke Bragg was in the lead again, going in short runs from cover to cover, his whole body tense, leaning forward a little, concentrating on the ride and not on the quarry. Cameron, fuming a little, followed on, but now he had to sheath his rifle and keep both hands free, for the going was getting much more difficult.

They reached the top of the farthest slope, and Luke Bragg checked up for a moment, staring keenly about him. There was no sign of the two men they were searching for, and Wilson Cameron swore. 'We should have run them killers down, damn it!'

'My way,' said Luke Bragg, without wasting words, then

suddenly surged his horse forward. 'I see them now! There they go!'

Dan Waters and Clint Murdoch were within a hundred or so yards of the two of them, riding at an easy lope down the gradual slope. They were not even aware of the approach of the other two men until Clint Murdoch, happening to turn his head, caught sight of them as they came pounding down. He let out a squawk of warning, then yanked his horse desperately to one side. Waters' reactions were quicker; almost before the sound had left Murdoch's lips, he had drawn his six gun. For a moment, Waters' horse obscured his view, and then, as Cameron came charging in, Waters cut loose with his six gun. The shot took Wilson Cameron in the shoulder, high up, and spun him from the saddle. Before he hit the ground, Luke Bragg went into action. Standing in the stirrups, he drew his gun while his horse was still galloping. He laid the barrel across his bent left arm and picked Waters off with a shot. Waters slumped over, with a neat hole dead centre of his forehead, was plucked out of the saddle, and then as his horse thrashed around his body was mangled to a pulp beneath the flying hoofs.

Luke Bragg was off his horse at a run. Clint Murdoch, a few yards away, hesitated for a moment. His indecision was his downfall. Bragg, aiming deliberately low, sent a bullet smashing into his left leg. With a squeal of rage and pain, Murdoch was spewed from his saddle. Bragg ran in, grabbed the trailing rein and with his gun menaced Murdoch who was sprawled in an ungainly position on the ground, his gun clear of his reach.

Then Wilson Cameron was there, staggering about

painfully, the blood leaking from his shoulder wound. He thrust past Bragg, and raised his six gun slowly until it was covering Murdoch's upturned face.

'Pray fast, boy! Pray fast, you mangy skunk!'

Blubbering, Murdoch appealed to Bragg. 'I can't die this way! I just can't!'

'Take it easy, Mr Cameron.' Bragg's tone was carefully measured. He knew Murdoch was within a hair's breadth of death. 'I want this man alive.'

There was hatred and anger on Cameron's face, and more than that, there was pain. 'This bastard killed my son!'

'I never done that!' Clint Murdoch attempted to get to his feet, protesting his innocence, but his smashed leg caved in under his weight and the pain, and he went sprawling.

'Mr Cameron, we have got to take this man in,' Luke Bragg said.

'He is as guilty as the other one over there,' Cameron said, throwing a quick nod in the direction of the body of Waters.

'I never kilt young Jack. I swear it! It was Dan!' Murdoch shouted.

'That was what the boy said before he died, Mr Cam— Wilson,' Bragg added.

'I am not caring about that,' snarled Cameron. 'It was Murdoch here who scattered the sheep – Clint Murdoch was in it, too. He is just as responsible for the murder of my boy!'

'And he will stand trial for it!' Bragg put his hand out carefully inched towards the outstretched gun. 'Believe me, Wilson, I know I am right about this.'

'This is my quarrel . . . you keep out of it, Bragg.' His face was ashen, his eyes intently staring.

'Listen to me, Wilson. This whole valley is against us. Kill this man – Murdoch – and you kill the only proof we have got of what really happened,' reasoned Bragg.

'You think I care about that now? The hell with this valley and the Cattlemen's Association, too! I don't care anything about my sheep – nor anything, except that I had a son, and how he's lost to me!'

Luke Bragg said in a firm voice, 'Listen good for the last time. Kill this man, and I tell you the ranchers will rise against you and they will have you hanged before another day is out.'

'The hell with—!'

'And your wife too, Cameron. You care nothing for her?' screamed Bragg.

At that Wilson Cameron whirled on him. 'What are you tryin' to prove, damn you?'

'Be guided. I tell you the dice is loaded against you and against me, too – and I guess against all the decent folks in this here valley. We know Murdoch had a hand in killing your boy. All right, we will show him to the people and make him tell—'

'You figger he will admit he is guilty?' Cameron gave a laugh that was almost a sob. 'You don't know the kind of skunks you are dealing with, Bragg – how could you know?' said Cameron.

'Men are the same the world over.' He turned his head a little so he could take in the man crouched on the ground. 'Murdoch – that is your name, right? Do you want to live?'

'Just give me a chance, mister. . . .'

'You ready to tell the truth about what happened back there?'

'Sure, I will tell—'

Wilson Cameron snarled, 'And let them hang you for it? I don't believe you, you lyin', no good polecat. . . .' Again the gun barrel, which had started to droop, jerked up and with that Luke Bragg flung himself forward slamming his hard palm into Cameron's gun hand, deflecting the six gun, which exploded in that instant, discharging its bullet harmlessly into the air.

'Damn you!' Cameron swung the gun, struck Bragg on the side of the head with it. The big man took the blow, then put up both hands, palms outward, against Cameron.

'Not now,' he said. 'Not now.'

'Damn you . . .' mouthed the homesteader once more, but he didn't strike out again.

Bragg stood very still for a few seconds, then said, without turning his head, 'Clint Murdoch, lie face down in the dirt.'

Without further ado, the Bar B rider flopped on his belly in the dirt. Luke Bragg dropped to one knee beside him, rapidly searched him, then, jerking his wrists behind his back, tied them with a thong he took from his belt. All the while Wilson Cameron stood staring at nothing.

'I guess you are safe to tote along,' said Bragg, and jerked Murdoch to his feet. The man whined.

'I can't stand on my leg. It's busted, thanks to you!'

Without a word, Bragg put his shoulder under the

man's armpit, dragged him over to his horse.

'Hell, I can't ride either!' spat Murdoch.

'You will or I will drag you from my horse,' Bragg said firmly. 'Your choice.'

Propping the man against him, Bragg stripped the horse of its saddle, then hoisted Murdoch across its back. He used Murdoch's lariat to lash him to the horse, passed the lariat end through the bridle piece, then hitched it to his own horse. He walked over to where Cameron still stood, starting at nothing.

'That shoulder of yours needs attention. You had best see a doctor.'

'Bullet went clear through, I guess,' groaned Cameron in a dreary voice, without looking at Bragg. 'Only a flesh wound.'

Luke Bragg was still concerned. 'You have bled a lot.'

'I will live.' Cameron faced Bragg. 'What do you aim to do with that no good varmint, Murdoch?'

'Take him to town,' replied Bragg.

'You are crazy.'

Luke Bragg shook his head. 'I don't think so. I am trusting to that sheriff you got in there.'

'Mick Gardner? He is all right, but he won't serve Murdoch as he should.'

'He won't hang him out of hand, if that is what you mean. But see here, Cameron, you had better get it into your head once and for all . . . this is a war we are fighting, not a private feud. We are going to use Murdoch, and that is the way it has to be.'

Their eyes clashed then, and Cameron was the first to turn his head. He muttered, 'I ain't comin' in with you.'

'You aren't going to back me in this?' Luke Bragg asked with shock.

'I sure ain't goin' to fool around with no law courts! I know who killed my son, and I know what ought to be done with this murdering no-good skunk. So you can count me out,' Cameron growled.

'I think you had best see to your wife, Cameron.'

'Leave me to mind my own affairs!' flared the homesteader, and then quite suddenly the mad anger died from his face. He said awkwardly, 'Got to go back to the mountain – go to get the body.'

'With that shoulder wound? See here, I will tell you what we will do. We will head back to your ranch, break the news to your wife,' Bragg said.

'Leave that for me to do,' Cameron replied softly.

'You figure I would horn in at a time like this? I only want to help you, Wilson.'

'I know,' muttered the other man, 'but I have got to get my boy.'

'We will get him. It isn't all that far back to your place. We will take Murdoch with us and shut him up where he can't escape and then come back for the bo . . . Jack.'

Cameron turned and stared at the man sprawled across the horse's back. He gave a hard laugh.

'With that leg he wouldn't get very far.'

'I know it. I also want to make him sweat a little.' He paused and added, 'That make you feel any better?'

'Nothin' will make me feel any better again.' He turned and spat. 'All right, then what do we do?'

'You got a wagon, or a flatbed buckboard or such?' asked Bragg.

'Yeah, I got a wagon and horses. Reckon we can use that to get Jack's body.'

'Guess so, Cameron. It is rough going. You'll need help, I'll come with you,' Bragg offered.

'Bragg – I don't know what to say – guess I ain't myself right now. . . .'

'You have to talk. Get your horse and mount up.'

Cameron shambled away to where his horse stood, its rein trapped under one hoof. Luke Bragg mounted up, taking the lead rein, and started out. They reached Cameron's homestead while there was still light and did all that there was to be done. Cameron's wife showed surprising strength in view of the terrible news they brought her. Without fuss, she set about bathing and tending the grumbling Cameron's wound. In the meantime, Bragg placed his prisoner in the woodshed. By the time they got back with Jack Cameron's body, dusk had fallen. But Bragg insisted on taking his prisoner into town, in spite of the hour. He even refused to have supper with the Camerons, and, leaving them to their grief, he set out for town, towing his prisoner behind him.

Four hours later, Hank Bonnadeen, boss of the Bar B, came thundering up to the Crazy 8 ranch house on a lathered horse, flung himself off, ran up the porch steps and rapped loudly on the door. He was admitted by the thin, frightened young wife of Rance Cash, the Bar B boss. One glance at his visitor's face, and Cash turned and led the way into the room he used as his office.

'I have whiskey in the closet,' he said, 'but first – I better hear your news, Hank.'

'It is the worst. I just came from town. Mick Gardner's holding one of my boys there – Clint Murdoch, one of my best riders. He is holding him for his part in the murder of Jack Cameron.' He paused, his eyes glittering in his pale face. 'One man brought him in, Rance. The man who killed Dan Waters—'

Rance Cash started forward, shouting, 'Dan Waters? My wrangler? What in hell's this you're giving me?'

'Hard truth. It seems you have had no news of Waters. . . .'

'All I know is he didn't show up this evening – my foreman spoke to me about it. We reckoned he must have gone on to town – he was always one with a taste for liquor, but what is this about him being killed?' demanded Rance.

'He was killed by the man who brought in my rider, Murdoch. Between them it is said they killed Jack Cameron.'

'Who brought him in?' snarled Cash.

'Give you a guess, my friend,' offered Bonnadeen.

They faced each other in silence. A nerve was jumping in Rance Cash's cheek. At last he grated out, 'It must be Luke Bragg!'

'Who else?' Hank Bonnadeen sketched a vague motion with his thin hands. 'We have had enough and to spare, Rance. He has got to die.'

'I will call up all my riders and with your bunch—'

'No.' Hank Bonnadeen shook his head. 'Not that way. It needs to be a quick and quiet killing.'

'Against Bragg's gun? We saw him in action against Carver.'

'He would have to be fast to best Clay.'

The silence hung between them. Then Rance Cash made a sound that was a mixture of laughter and jeering.

'And how do we get Lee Clay, the gun? Do we wave a magic wand or some damn thing? Conjure him up out of thin air?'

'We don't have to go to that much trouble,' said Bonnadeen, and now the silkiness was back in his voice. 'Clay rode with John Cannon, but he escaped Mick Gardner when the big round-up was made. Clay escaped into the hills and only came out when it suited him.'

'When it suited us,' corrected Rance Cash grimly.

'Don't let's fool around with words, my friend. Clay is in touch,' Bonnadeen stated.

'He went away a month ago,' exploded Cash. 'He went north.'

'You are wrong,' said Hank Bonnadeen. 'He was at Jackson Springs last week, trying to raise friends – and funds.'

Rance Cash stuck his big head forward like an inquisitive turtle. 'Why is this the first I am hearing of this?'

'The Wild Boys – Clay and his bunch – have an idea they can spring their old leader from the pen,' Bonnadeen remarked.

'Why, that is a fool plan,' said Cash. 'That will never work – will it? It is crazy!'

'We know it is crazy – but would the authorities?' Bonnadeen gave a thin laugh. 'But that is all by the way. Rest assured Lee Clay is in touch.'

Rance Cash leaned back in his chair. 'You can reach him?'

'Sure can,' Hank said with a grin. 'Within twenty-four hours.'

'Then get him,' rapped Rance Cash, and the veins stood out like cords in his temples.

CHAPTER 7

Sheriff Mick Gardner turned the key in the cell lock and moved away to face Luke Bragg.

'I am holding him for the night,' he said. 'That is all.'

'No longer?'

'All depends, Bragg,' the sheriff paused, eyeing the tall man in the lamplight. 'The doc says his leg will mend. Too bad the same can't be said for young Jack Cameron.'

Luke Bragg replied, 'Now we will see how much justice there is around Preston Gulch.'

'Bragg, I will get to the bottom of this. It is my business to do so. But I have got a word of warning for you,' the sheriff cautioned.

'Go ahead,' invited Bragg.

'This could easily start another range war. I would do most anything to stop that happening,' explained the sheriff.

'I don't think you would cover anything up just for the sake of peace and quiet, Sheriff,' Luke Bragg said.

'Did I say that?' Sheriff Gardner gave a short laugh. 'You have maybe got the wrong idea about me, Bragg.

Anyway, it doesn't matter. The point is, I don't aim to let you raise hell around my town.'

Bragg said steadily, 'To date, the only hell that has been raised has been against me.'

'So you say.'

'You aim to argue on that, Sheriff?' asked Bragg, dumbfounded.

Sheriff Mick Gardner gave a weary sigh, and moved over to his desk.

'Now see here, Bragg. Get one thing straight. Any time I have a mind to, I can move you on.'

Bragg's eyes narrowed. 'What is your drift, Gardner?'

'This is a big country but the telegraph kind of makes it smaller, you understand?' the sheriff replied coolly.

'No, explain it to me. What does that mean?' Bragg was getting frustrated now with the lawman.

'A friend of mine is a United States Marshal over in Jackson Springs. He keeps me wise on a whole lot of things. Got it into his head that maybe you were a man to be mindful of – a man to keep an eye on, if you will. He knew you were coming up here and put me on my guard, as you might say.' The sheriff paused, then went on, 'You got cleared of that killing back in Jackson Springs, and besides, I am not your judge and jury. But I have got to play it careful.'

'Don't blame you,' offered Luke Bragg, and his tone was calm now. 'But just by the way of interest – what do you know about that killing I was cleared of?'

'I don't know any more than what was sent to me by telegraph – just the bare facts that you had been cleared and were on your way up here – to Preston Gulch.' Again he paused, his eyes searching the other man's face.

'I don't have to square myself with you,' Bragg shot out. 'But I will tell you just this. I killed York because he was a no-good cheat and a liar and a thief. He killed a friend of mine and ruined the life of the woman who was fool enough to marry him. I am not going into any details; there is no call for me to explain myself, but I am lucky to be alive today – and I will tell you why. The jury was stacked against me because George York had a lot of friends in all the right places. He was that kind of man. But like I said, I was lucky – I dodged the rope and got clear. I have got nothing on my conscience.'

Sheriff Mick Gardner said quietly, 'I wouldn't want you to feel bitter over this. . . .'

Luke Bragg gave a short laugh. 'I am not bitter, Sheriff. What happened at Jackson Springs is over and done with. What is happening right now, here in Preston Gulch, is the thing that concerns us, or should do at any rate.'

'Tally it up for yourself,' said Gardner briskly. 'You come up here with a reputation. Right off, there is trouble—'

'None of my own making,' Bragg interrupted.

'I will give you that much,' the sheriff acknowledged, 'but the very fact is you are here, and already two men are dead. You cannot deny those facts.'

'It could have been me both times,' Bragg answered, with a good-humoured grin. 'But see here, what are you trying to prove?'

'I wear a badge and I try to live up to the responsibilities that come along with it.'

'As far as it goes, just dandy! But don't bust your back

leaning over trying to please everybody,' Bragg replied.

Sheriff Mick Gardner snapped, 'You tryin' to teach me how to do my job, Bragg?'

'That would be the last idea I would have. But you have put me on a spot where I have got to apologize almost for breathing!'

'You know it isn't like that – all I was. . . .'

'Just because you want to keep the peace. . . .' Bragg started to say.

'Anything wrong with that, Bragg? You are forgetting this town was a mess when I took over! I am not braggin' but someone had to use an iron hand,' the sheriff explained.

'And you were that man,' nodded Bragg. 'Again fair enough. You had a ranchers' war, and now it has flared up again. It so happens I am caught up in it. There is no call for grief on you part – just so long as you don't get things kinda tangled.'

'Meaning exactly what?' snapped the sheriff.

'You can't ride with the ranchers and keep the peace. You can't take the side of the sheepherders – not even poor old Cameron who lost his son. That would mean open warfare with the big ranchers who carry all the weight around this territory. The townsmen, I guess, go either way as it suits them. But, believe me, Sheriff, you will never have peace around here until you get your sights on the right target,' Luke Bragg said firmly.

'Maybe you can tell me just what that target is?'

'Maybe I sound like I am trying to teach you your job but – to me, a stranger coming in, it seems plain as day that the cattle ranchers are in the wrong here,' Bragg said.

'Naturally you would take that view—'

'On account of my uncle?' Luke Bragg shook his head. 'Not only that. I think I am fair minded – and at least I am neutral!'

'But you have inherited the spread – a good ranch—'

'That doesn't put me on the side of the sheepherders – they no longer exist anyway! Why should I worry over the bad talk there was about the killing of Ben Flynn? The fact that my uncle's name was used in that talk – why should that worry me either? He is dead. Like you said, I have inherited – and right now I could turn my sheep off and become a cattle rancher, just like Hank Bonnadeen and Rance Cash! I could join the Association and come to town in a nice clean shirt every Saturday and hell it up with the boys!' He paused. 'Well, Sheriff? Why don't I do that?'

'I was about to ask you that same question, Bragg.'

'Maybe because I have got a crazy notion that those ranchers had no right to haze my uncle and all the other sheepherders around here! Maybe I don't go along with smoking homesteaders out, and forcing simple sheepmen to quit!'

The sheriff sighed. 'Now, see here. . . !'

'Maybe I am just cussed! I don't like being braced on the open range by big-mouthed, arrogant men. Carver died because he took me cheap. Maybe he was faster than me – but he just didn't try! So he died and—'

'And now another man is dead,' interjected Mick Gardner. He was no longer frowning, but staring at the floor.

'That cowpuncher died because he was a coyote! Do I

97

have to make excuses for stomping on his breed?' Luke Bragg was in a fine fettle, raging along like a torrent. 'Young Jack Cameron never asked for a bullet – his sheep didn't ask to be pushed over a cliff! For Pete's sake, Sheriff, where does all this end? In surrender to these arrogant ranchers – the wiping out of all sheepherders and simple little men? Where do you want to wind up? President of the Cattlemen's Association, or maybe with a spread of your own, so you can lord it around like Cash and Bonnadeen? Is that what you are after?'

Sheriff Mick Gardner looked up. He said mildly, 'I never picked you for a loose mouth, Bragg.'

Luke Bragg flushed, then gave an angry laugh. 'Guess you prodded me into shooting wild – and that isn't like me! I will take that back about your ambitions—'

'Great. But I don't give a damn one way or another! I know what I am here for, and what I aim to do. I am leaving you run, Bragg, but you had best stick around town until tomorrow. Get yourself a room at the hotel. With Waters dead and Murdoch behind bars there, the ranchers are going to put a torch to the brush any time now. We had best get ready to fight a forest fire.'

Hank Bonnadeen stood at the counter of the telegraph depot. While Cam Taplow, the operator, watched him curiously from the other side, he read again the message he had carefully penned for transmission to the man named Langford who ran a rooming house in Jackson Springs. Langford was to be trusted. For years he had provided a hideout for John Cannon and his friends – and those friends included Lee Clay, the gun.

URGENTLY REQUIRE THE GUN.
WILL PAY ONE THOUSAND DOLLARS' CASH ON
ARRIVAL.

It was signed Hank Bonnadeen.

The rancher handed the slip of paper across the counter. 'Send this right away, Taplow, in care of Langford, Main Street, Jackson Springs.'

'Just like you say, Mr Bonnadeen.' The operator took the message, glanced through it perfunctorily and then turned his startled eyes on Bonnadeen. 'You want that this goes out just like it says here?'

'That is the way you usually send messages, isn't it?' Hank Bonnadeen answered, annoyed.

'Yeah, but . . .' Cam Taplow scratched his head. 'This means you are offering to pay a thousand dollars in cash for a shooting iron! This must be some kind of joke. . . .'

'Do I look like I am in a joking mood, Taplow?' said Bonnadeen smoothly, and leaned his forearms on the counter in a confiding manner. 'That gun is a very valuable weapon. It was made by Sam Colt himself – for the Governor of New Mexico.'

'You don't say.'

'I collect valuable guns of that sort. It so happens that I have one to match it. I need this gun of Langford's to match up the pair, you see. But, you keep this to yourself, Taplow. You understand?'

'Guess so, but—'

'I wouldn't want any of my rivals to know that I was after this gun. Rance Cash, now – or the sheriff! They are men who like a good gun. If they get to hear of this, they might horn in on the deal,' Bonnadeen said calmly.

Again Cam Taplow scratched his head and stared at the message. 'I won't spread it around – I ain't no gabber! But it seems to me these days a man's got to keep his mouth like a shut bear-trap if anything interesting comes into the depot.'

'This might help keep the bear trap locked,' said Bonnadeen, and tossed a five-dollar bill on the counter.

Cam Taplow stared at the bill, then slowly picked it up. 'Ain't no call for this, Mr Bonnadeen, but thank you kindly just the same.'

'You are welcome.' Bonnadeen added, 'Don't tell me I am the only one sending confidential messages away these days?'

'Sure ain't!' exploded Taplow, as he tucked away the five-dollar bill. 'Trouble is, Sheriff Gardner ain't so generous. Fact is, he sticks his durned jaw out at me, and tells me to keep quiet or else!'

There was a sudden spark of interest in Bonnadeen's eyes. He said, with a smile, 'I will bet that five dollars I know what Gardner wanted you to keep quiet about.'

Taplow protested, 'I ain't no betting man, Mr Bonnadeen, but . . .'

'Come on now! Gardner and I are good friends, and there is precious little goes on in this town that I don't know about. Have a small bet with me, Taplow.'

The operator shook his head vigorously, shaking loose the eyeshade that dropped ludicrously over one brow.

'You would never guess it, Mr Bonnadeen. Though I am durned if I know why he was makin' such a hell of a secret of it. He often gets messages from the marshal down at Jackson Springs.'

Bonnadeen hooded his eyes. He said with a little laugh, 'I know all about that marshal. He and Gardner are thick as thieves – though it is hardly the right word to use about two such excellent lawmen. But I still think I would win that bet.'

Cam Taplow said, 'What would I want to go gab about it for, anyway? Ain't none of my affair – though they do say this Luke Bragg aims to make a whole lotta trouble around these parts.'

Hank Bonnadeen said softly, 'I am sure I would have won that bet if you would have only given me the chance! Luke Bragg – it had to be. . . .'

'You guessed it? Well, now – I reckon you do know about most of the things that are goin' on around here, Mr Bonnadeen! But if Bragg was cleared of that killing in Jackson Springs, why would the marshal be warning Sheriff Gardner about him?'

'You have a fine point there, Taplow,' said Bonnadeen.

'Yeah, yeah, I sure have.' Taplow cleared his throat importantly. 'What I want to know is, why in hell get mean with me like the sheriff done? Seems to me he is getting too high and mighty these days.'

'Well, I suppose he has to do his job,' said Bonnadeen in a tolerant tone. 'If Luke Bragg is a wanted man, he has to be on his guard, I guess. It makes sense for the local sheriff to know these things.'

'Yeah, yeah, but Gardner don't have to be so durned secretive about it! Seems to me if this Bragg is so danger-ous, the whole town should know!' said Taplow.

'I believe you are right there, Mr Taplow,' said Hank Bonnadeen sagely. 'Ours is only a small community, and we can't afford to let a wild man loose among us.'

Taplow said eagerly, 'You know about this Luke Bragg, Mr Bonnadeen?'

'I know all about Luke Bragg,' replied the cattle rancher. 'He killed a man down at Jackson Springs and got away with it. Now he's killed again. . . .'

'Yeah, I heard about poor Seth Carver! Cut down cold, they reckon,' said Taplow with conviction.

'And he is not the only one,' added Bonnadeen. 'Today he killed another cowpoke – man named Waters, rode for the Crazy 8.'

'Dan Waters!' Cam Taplow was bug-eyed. 'I knew him well! Bragg killed him, huh?'

'In cold blood,' said Bonnadeen. 'Seems to me it is high time the sheriff came right out in the open about this killer – what do you say, Taplow?'

Cam Taplow nodded so energetically his eyeshade fell down over his ears. 'You are dead right, Mr Bonnadeen! Why cover up for this mangy killer? We oughta get the skunk and hang him sky high!'

'Maybe we will do just that, Taplow.' Hank Bonnadeen straightened, smiled enigmatically down into the flushed face of the telegraph operator. 'It could be that we will see the end of Mr Luke Bragg very soon – and that would be a good thing for the whole of Preston Gulch.'

CHAPTER 8

Lena Flynn drove a light wagon to the town trail from Sunrise. It was a cold morning and the sky was leaden, as if filled with the gloomy promise of snow to come. Huddled in warm clothing on the seat of the rig, the girl shivered a little. She had a feeling of heaviness, of depression. But from time to time her thoughts strayed to the man who had come as a stranger to the valley and brought with him grief.

She steered the rig down on to the flat land, forcing herself to think not of Luke Bragg but of the things she had to do in town. Tim Sennett, the lawyer, had not been out to see her in several days, which was unlike the faithful Tim. She was not concerned over that, but over the papers she had to show him; papers she had unearthed in her patient cleaning up of her father's desk and bureau drawers.

She was jerked violently out of her reverie by the sight of old Tramp Eckelmann who, on foot, was attempting to force a young steer out of a patch of brush. He was so intent on his work that he failed to notice the approach of the rig until it was almost on top of him. Then he turned a sweating face and called cheerfully, 'Did you ever see a more ornery critter?'

Angrily, Lena called, 'Is that one of my steers you have got there?'

'Sure has your brand on it, Miss Lena!' He jerked a thumb at the exploding sun burnt into the young steer's hide. 'Fine lookin' critter, too, though ornery.'

'Have you taken to rustling my cattle as well?'

Tramp's face clouded. 'As well as what? What do you mean, Miss Lena?'

'It seems you Black Hills people will stop at nothing these days!' Lena shouted back.

'Durn it!' exploded Tramp. 'One thing we do stop at, and that is rustling, miss!'

'Then what are you doing with my steer?'

'I ain't polishing its mangy hide!' retorted the old man. 'I rode down the town trail, and seen this critter was through a wire. Got itself holed up in the brush here. Got its fool head caught and—'

'All right,' broke in Lena impatiently. 'Free it!'

'Miss Lena,' said the old man, his beard jutting, 'if I wasn't a gent and raised that way, I would tell you to go plumb to hell and free it yourself.'

'It is what I would expect from you,' she replied.

'What in blazes has gotten into you?' Tramp Eckelmann exclaimed. 'We was always friends, you and me, Miss Lena! Now you are treatin' me like I was a no good, mangy skunk!'

'I think it is very strange that I should find you on this side of the wire with one of my steers. . . .'

'Well, I wasn't tryin' to rustle it off,' bellowed Rufus, snatching off his hat and dashing it to the ground. 'And only a fool woman with no brains in her head would think different!'

'Be careful,' she warned him, her eyes sparking. 'Don't go too far, old man!'

'Mebbe I am old, but I still got a few wits left in my head, which is more'n can be said about some folks! All right, Miss Lena, be mean – go right ahead and get bitter with all your old friends and see how you like it!'

Suddenly Lena's eyes filled with tears. Choking a bit, she said, 'You didn't take my part in the sheriff's office that night. You let those men ride clear over me!'

'Now, see here, Miss Lena—'

'What's more, you took their part! You attacked me, just as they did.'

'So that's the trouble!' Rufus munched his gums for a moment of silence, and then, 'Guess we got our trails tangled there, Miss Lena. I never had nothing against you – and I figgered your old man was the whitest. But I am workin' on Luke Bragg's payroll now—'

'And whatever he says goes. Is that it? No matter what he does, who he hurts – it is all right with you! Just so long as the money's good!' she said, hurt.

'Now that ain't fair one bit, Miss Lena. I stuck to old man Bragg through all the trouble – your old man made some of that trouble for him, too! Don't you go forgettin' that!'

'Sheepmen and cattlemen never mix . . .'

'The hell with that,' exploded Tramp. 'Ain't no reason why both sorts shouldn't live peaceable on a range the size of this, I reckon.'

'I am not going to argue with you—'

'You are if I say so!' He clutched at the wheel, glaring up at her. 'Time you got a little sense in that purty head of yours! You got the wrong idea about Bragg when Carver was killed – if ever there was a no-account polecat, Seth Carver was it.'

'I tell you—'

'You ain't tellin' me nothin', Miss Lena! Carver was a polecat and I can prove it a hundred times over! He was a bully and a cheat. I reckon Ben Flynn wouldn't have put him on his payroll if it hadn't been for Hank Bonnadeen and that fast talkin' gent from Jackson Springs – what was his name? Lander or some such—'

'Carl Langford?' Lena's eyes were suddenly wide. 'It is strange that you should mention his name, Mr Eckelmann.'

'Ain't strange at all,' growled the old man. 'I remember when Lander or Langford came up here, a few months back it was, and Carver was with him. Langford was a real townsman, but he was with Hank Bonnadeen and Rance Cash and that made it all right with your old man, I reckon. Trouble with straight shooters like Ben Flynn, they never kin see the bad in others.'

'Stop straying off the point, Mr Eckelmann! Or, better still, stop talking and let me think for a minute,' the girl said.

'What you got to think about? You got your mind made up about Seth Carver – and I am only remindin' you that he was a stranger – only came in on the say-so of that Langford fella, or Lander, or what the hell! Don't know what there was between Bonnadeen and Langford, but Bonnadeen was sure keen and eager to have Flynn hire Carver that time,' Rufus explained.

Lena stared wide-eyed at the old man. 'How do you know so much about this?'

'I was around,' retorted Tramp. 'It was before the cattlemen started gettin' tough with Oscar Bragg, and everybody was friends! I was down there at the corrals when Ben Flynn talked with them others, and Carver was hangin' around with that silly grin on his face all the while.' He grumbled to himself for a moment, then burst out, 'Always did reckon there was somethin' funny about Seth Carver. He hadn't been around more'n a few weeks when he picked a fight with some poor jasper in town and beat the ears off'n him just for the hell of it! He was a mean and nasty s—'

'All right, all right,' said Lena Flynn angrily. 'You have made your point!'

Tramp's mouth fell open. At last he managed to say, 'You mean you – you think Carver had it comin' to him? The way he was killed, I mean?'

'I am certainly not taking your word for what happened – nor Hank Bonnadeen's for that matter! I am quite open-minded about the whole thing.'

'Your mind's so durned open, a bunch of cows could drift through—'

He broke off with a yell as the Sunrise steer, having quietly freed itself from the wire and brush while the two were talking, retreated rapidly from the brush, struck the old man from behind and sent him sprawling. The woman burst out laughing as Tramp scrambled to his feet and started after the steer, cussing it heartily. By the time he had got back, Lena's laughter had subsided, but it was as if the incident had relieved some of the tension in her.

'That was a judgment on you, Tramp,' she said. 'Now, pick up your hat and stop looking so foolish.'

'Only one good thing about it,' he told her, as he reached for his hat. 'You just lost yourself a good steer!'

'We will get him back some day. He doesn't matter . . . Rufus, forget about the steer.'

'Reckon the sheriff's still nosing around tryin' to get the truth about that shootin'. But as far as I am concerned, Carver's dead and that's the end of it,' the old man said.

'And now there has been fresh trouble,' said the woman gravely.

The old timer nodded. 'Just got the news of the Camerons' loss,' he said grimly. 'That is why I am headin' for town.' He jerked is head towards the trail. 'Jumped off my horse to go into the brush. I got him tied up there. You headin' for town, Miss Lena?'

'Yes, I am.' She paused for a moment thoughtfully, then, 'Why isn't Luke Bragg with you?'

'He ain't showed up. The way I heard it he gunned down Dan Waters, took Clint Murdoch prisoner, toted him to the sheriff. Guess he has stayed in town with his prisoner,' Tramp said.

'Just what sort of man is he, Mr Eckelmann?' the woman asked.

'Young, white and American,' replied the old man, with a toothless grin, at which Lena frowned.

'It's plain I won't get any sense out of you!' she said sharply, and gathered up her reins. 'If you do see your Mr

Bragg, tell him from me he had better not start bringing his war onto the Sunrise! I may be only a woman, but I can protect myself and my interests!'

'Bet you can,' he said promptly, 'and I sure will pass on your message, Miss Lena. He sure will be glad to hear from you – the way he talked after you met up with him in town, he was real struck by you!'

In the act of driving away she turned swiftly, her eyes wide. 'Did he say that?'

'Sure did,' lied Tramp. 'Said you were the purtiest female he had sighted in years! Mebbe ever.'

She was certain the old man was just saying those things to make her feel better; she said nothing as she drove off, leaving Tramp grinning.

Hank Bonnadeen faced Sheriff Mick Gardner across the law office desk. 'Are you trying to stop me from seeing your prisoner?'

'You are welcome to see him any time, Bonnadeen.' The sheriff's tone was uncompromising. 'He is right back there, and you can see him plain through the bars.'

'You know perfectly well what I mean, Sheriff! I want to talk with Murdoch – after all, he is one of my riders—'

'And I am not stopping you from talking to him,' broke in Sheriff Gardner. 'Through the bars with me right alongside you.'

The rancher's thin face flushed angrily. 'Just what are you holding him on – might I ask?'

'You are entitled to,' replied Gardner politely. 'I have reason to believe he was concerned in the shooting of Jack Cameron.'

'What reason? On whose witness?'

Sheriff Gardner hesitated a moment and then said, 'Luke Bragg.' He added, 'As you already know, I would reckon.'

'I also well know that Bragg's word is not worth a damn,' snapped Bonnadeen.

'I take it you can back that statement up, Mr Bonnadeen?'

'I don't have to back anything up!' The rancher was getting very hostile.

'You are dead wrong there, Mr Bonnadeen.'

'I tell you, you can't take the word of that no-account drifter! He has already killed one man in cold blood – and nearly killed Clint here. It looks like Bragg's running true to his record, wouldn't you say, Sheriff?'

Gardner's eyes narrowed but he said nothing.

'It is true, isn't it, that Bragg's already stood trial for murder?' asked the rancher.

'All I know about Bragg is that he was acquitted of whatever he was supposed to have done in Jackson Springs.'

Hank Bonnadeen gave a contemptuous laugh. 'Now you are showing your hand, Sheriff! It is plain that you are on his side. Well, for your information, I don't intend to let Bragg get away with any more bloodletting! Not in my town!'

'And what do you propose to do about it?' asked the lawman.

'You will see!' The rancher got to his feet, stood slim and menacing, looking down at the sheriff. 'There are going to be some awkward questions asked of you in the next twenty-four hours. Best be ready with the answers.'

He turned and started to march towards the door. Gardner got up, moved around the desk and caught up with Bonnadeen as he put his hand on the door latch.

'Hold it right there, Mr Bonnadeen.'

The rancher swung swiftly to face the sheriff.

'Just what do you think you are doing?'

'Come back and take a chair. Let's get two or three things straightened out before you go running off,' the sheriff explained.

'I am through with talking, I tell you. I am off and you can't hold me!'

'I could, you know.' Gardner's voice was deceptively soft. But Bonnadeen wasn't deceived.

'What the devil are you driving at?' he said sharply.

'Luke Bragg wasn't the only one to lay information against Clint Murdoch. I already talked with Wilson Cameron – he hit town before noon.'

'And what has that sheepherder to do with me?'

'Just this, Bonnadeen. Cameron's story tallies exactly with Bragg's. He told me just what he found out there on the mountain and just what his son said to him before he died. It tallied word for word,' the sheriff explained.

'Naturally,' sneered Bonnadeen. 'Cameron has everything to gain by concocting a story and sticking to it, Sheriff!'

'I am accepting his story, Mr Bonnadeen. And from there I asked myself one question: whose idea was it to drive those sheep over the cliff?'

Hank Bonnadeen was staring at him, his nostrils slightly dilated.

'Clint Murdoch wouldn't have enough brains to come

in out of the wet. He was way off his territory and so was his sidekick Dan Waters. They ambushed young Jack Cameron – that's as plain as all get out. I know that part of the trail – I know how Cameron and Bragg must have ridden round the spur to pick up the bunch of sheep when it got through the narrow defile. I know just the place where those two bushwhackers hid – timing it so they had Jack on his own and could get to work on the flock of sheep.' Again he paused, but Bonnadeen was still silent, his eyes staring. 'They were put up to that, Bonnadeen. Who was it? Rance Cash or you?'

'Why, damn you. . . !'

'Take it very easy!' Sheriff Mick Gardner's hand did not move, but there was menace in every inch of him. 'I am laying it right on the line for you. Either you or Cash or both wanted to make certain sure Luke Bragg got no more sheep for Black Hills, so Waters and Murdoch were sent out because Bragg's a hard man with a gun. Too bad about young Jack Cameron! If there is any justice in this state, Murdoch will go to the pen for twenty years.'

Bonnadeen fumbled for the door latch. He was shaking. He jerked out, 'Just as well there are no witnesses – just as well no one was around to hear you lay that foul accusation against me.'

The sheriff glared back at the rancher. 'Deny it, Bonnadeen.'

'I am denying nothing!'

'You want that I charge you, that it?' the sheriff threw out.

At that Hank Bonnadeen spun and his right hand clawed inside his jacket. Instantly Gardner's left hand shot out, gripping the wiry wrist, holding it in a grip of steel.

'What do you want, Bonnadeen? A hard trail to the pen? Or maybe a pine box?'

White as death, the rancher mumbled, 'I meant no harm – Sheriff.'

'Nobody goes to draw on me, Bonnadeen. Not even you – big as you are!' The lawman released his grip on the other's wrist, reached past him and threw open the door. 'Get on your way, Bonnadeen. We have had our talk and now you have seen the cards I am holding. Murdoch goes up for trail and – one last warning. Make a false move, one of you bloody-minded ranchers, and I will turn this town inside out to get you! I give you good day, Mr Bonnadeen.'

Blindly, the rancher stumbled out into the grey daylight. Mick Gardner watched him go, then with sudden decision, he reached for his hat, and, as he went out of the office, he hitched up his gun belt.

CHAPTER 9

In another part of town Lena Flynn sat in conference with Tim Sennett. They were in his back office with the door closed, and under any circumstances Tim would have glowed at the thought of her presence and her closeness to him. But the matter in hand was too serious even for the ardent Tim. He sat at his desk with Ben Flynn's private papers spread before him and stacked in deed boxes to one side. Across the desk, Lena sat eagerly on the edge of her chair.

'I suppose there is no possibility of a mistake?' There was a tremor of excitement in her voice.

Sennett, staring down at the papers, shook his head slowly. 'There could be no mistake, Lena. Your father was a very methodical man and he wrote everything down. Those papers . . .' He tapped the desk. 'These papers are pages he intended to file in the books he kept specially for the purpose.'

'These journals I found,' nodded Lena, lightly touching the vellum back of one of the thick volumes piled on the desk. 'I had no idea that he kept a diary.'

'It was more than that. It was a sort of journal – all that happened to him and his affairs in connection with the ranch.' He looked up with a half smile. 'Your father was a remarkable man, Lena. One day, perhaps, we will get all the journals together and make his life story out of them.'

'You mean publish them?' Lena smiled to him, but shook her head slightly. 'I don't think I would ever want to do that. For one thing, I am quite sure my father never had that in mind.'

'I am not so sure,' said Sennett. 'After all, he made sure his journals wouldn't go astray. As he filled each set of loose pages, he gathered it together and bound it with his own hands in those patent folders.' He nodded towards the thick books. 'What I am trying to say is he went to no end of trouble to keep his journals for posterity.'

'I am quite sure that wasn't his intention,' replied Lena positively. 'He was just that kind of man. He loved method and order in everything he did. And quite obviously he hated throwing anything away! You have no idea the amount of junk I went through in those closets in his office back home at Sunrise. He even kept bills of accounts dating back thirty years.' She moved on her chair. 'Tim – Mr Sennett – what are we going to do with these journals?'

Tim Sennett smoothed a hand carefully over one of the open pages before him. At last he said, 'You realize just what these later notes imply?'

'From what I read – and from what you read out – it is plain that my father discovered a conspiracy.'

'Among the other ranchers,' noted the lawyer, nodding as he spoke.

'With Rance Cash as the ringleader, and Hank Bonnadeen not far behind,' said the woman.

'Careful,' cautioned Sennett, glancing nervously at the door. 'This kind of talk is highly inflammable—'

'Not half as inflammable as those papers under your hand!' the woman retorted, without lowering her voice. 'Surely we are not likely to be overheard in here, Mr Sennett?'

'I trust not.' Tim Sennett still seemed nervous. His hand shook a little as he straightened the pages on the desk. 'It seems unbelievable that men of such standing should stoop to swindling and stealing—'

'And rustling their neighbour's cattle!' There was the light of battle in Lena's eyes, and she sat up in her chair as if ready to take action that very moment. 'When I think of how my father trusted those men! I know he always respected them for what they had, and for what they had achieved. Bonnadeen especially. He always said Cash was a man of great education, a credit to the cattle country.' She gave a hard laugh. 'How disillusioned he must have been when he found all this out!'

Tim Sennett said, 'For the life of me I don't know what to do, Lena.'

'I know what I shall do, right away.'

He looked up at her quickly, a question in his eyes.

'I shall take these journals away and read them right through,' said the woman, but Sennett jumped to his feet first.

'I couldn't allow that!'

'What? But Mr Sennett – I brought those journals to you – along with the other papers – and. . . .'

'In the old valise in the bottom of your rig!' The lawyer passed a hand over his forehead. 'When I think of the risk you ran!'

'I wasn't aware of the importance of the papers until I got them in here,' she admitted a little abashed, 'but as for the risk – no one but us two has any idea of the existence of the journals.'

'You may be right – but we can't be sure, and it is a very big secret to share, Lena.'

She measured him silently for a moment, and then, 'I am hoping it won't be too big for you, Mr Sennett.'

His thin cheeks flushed. He said awkwardly, 'I may not be much of a man, Lena. I have been a drunkard and worse. You and your father brought me back to decency and some sort of manhood at least. But whatever I have been – whatever I might have been – I know I could never hurt you.'

'Dear Tim.' She got to her feet as he moved round the desk to meet her, and laid her hands on his half raised arms. 'You will carry the secret all right, Tim. And when the time comes, you will get all the papers in order and present your case against the ranchers – showing them up in the eyes of the world for what they are.'

'At least,' said Sennett, 'we know your father was killed.'

'Yes, of course, but . . .' she broke off and suddenly her hands fell to her sides and her colour changed. 'Tim, he was killed because of what he knew. . . .' She stopped and the words hung in the air for a moment – a long moment.

Then the lawyer said deliberately, 'It has just struck you?'

'Of course that is why he was killed! Now I am beginning to wonder if it wasn't Seth Carver who did the actual killing – the man who was supposed to have found him dead!' Lena's hand flew to her throat.

'Carver's dead,' Sennett reminded her. 'But – we must not start speculating and making wild guesses! Such thoughts are dangerous.'

'Tim, what are we going to do?'

'If the ranchers were aware that your father knew about them – if he taxed Hank Bonnadeen with his information – and that is why he was killed – you are in danger too,' the lawyer noted.

'Are you trying to frighten me, Tim?' the woman said.

'My dear!' He put an arm on her shoulder. 'That is the very last thing I want! But we must face reality! That is why I insist that you leave all these papers here.'

'Are you wanting to play the hero, Tim?' she asked banteringly, and seeing the hurt expression on his face, added quickly, 'Don't mind me. I am so excited; I really don't know what I am saying. But of course you are correct. About the papers, I mean. They must stay here, locked up. You have a strongbox?'

'Of course. The safe over there. But perhaps we should take Mick Gardner into our confidence about all of this,' suggested the lawyer.

She nodded. 'I think it would be a good idea for you to take the sheriff into our confidence. I would feel easier in my mind, if you didn't have to carry the burden all on your own.'

Sennett said, 'I will talk with him. I feel that this is too big for any of us to handle here. I must get advice.'

'Advice, from whom, Tim?' Lena inquired.

'There is an attorney in Jackson Springs, a man named

Jessup. He has handled cases for the railroad corporation – even had to go to Washington one time. I would like to talk with him on this matter,' answered Sennett.

'That would mean you would have to confide in him, wouldn't it?'

Tim Sennett gave a short laugh. 'Naturally! But you must understand, Lena, just how big all this is. It isn't just a matter of going out and filing an indictment against Cash and Bonnadeen and the other ranchers. The conspiracy's so big it will have to go to the highest court in the land.'

'And in the meantime?' she asked.

'We must go very cautiously. I suggest you go back to the ranch and . . . don't discuss this with anyone!'

'As if I would! But how about you?' she wanted to know.

'I will take the stage tomorrow to Jackson Springs and see Jessup.'

'And what of the sheriff, Tim?'

'I will talk to him today,' he replied.

CHAPTER 10

The night stage from Jackson Springs carried only two passengers for Preston Gulch, one a drummer selling a line of soft goods, and the other a slim, dark, almost insignificant man, registered on the manifest as Mason, and notable only for the lightness of his valise. The stage set down its passengers outside the freight office on Main, where horses were changed for the stage through to Perry. It was this coach that Tim Sennett planned to take on its return journey the following day, through Preston Gulch to Jackson Springs.

The drummer staggered away with his bulging baggage and the man who called himself Mason picked up his small valise and walked into the freight office. He waited patiently until the freight clerk paused his labours before addressing him.

'Where do I find the livery stable, friend?'

The clerk looked vague for a moment, and then said, 'Why, I guess Emerson Tolen's place is just off Main a couple of blocks – turn left when you pass the saloon.' As if seeing the other for the first time, he added, 'You just off the stage, mister?'

'I handed in my ticket when I stepped down. The name's Mason,' the stranger grumbled.

'Oh, yeah, yeah . . . say now, you from Jackson Springs?'

'That's right. What's it to you?'

'Mebbe you are the gent who was expected. There is a message for you,' the clerk explained.

The man calling himself Mason narrowed his eyes. He said cautiously, 'What sort of message?'

'From Hank Bonnadeen, of the Crazy 8. He called by here an hour ago. Said he was expecting a gun from Jackson Springs – figgered mebbe you are the gent totin' it for him,' answered the clerk.

'That would be key-rect,' said Mason. 'I am the man.'

'Great. It slipped my mind when the stage came in – I got a dozen things to think of, and a man ain't double-headed. Say, now, Mr Bonnadeen said this gun was valuable. You a drummer for Colts, mister?'

'You could say that I am. But what was the message?' prompted the man calling himself Mason.

'Mr Bonnadeen, he just said if you came in on the stage to drop by the Cattlemen's Association. That is the office down past the feed store.'

'Reckon I can find it,' said Mason gravely. 'I am obliged to you.'

'You are most welcome,' said the clerk, and bustled off to get the coach under way.

Mason made his way slowly up the street, looking neither to the left or the right. His clothing was as non-committal as his general appearance. The air was bitterly cold, but he wore no heavy coat, just a short jacket with the sheepskin turned in to his body, above the pants men used to call 'California brush breakers'. He wore only one gun and that was tied down, but not obtrusively, the thongs securing it to his thigh, laced at the back to keep the oil-smooth holster secure.

In spite of the cold there were a lot of people about. From one saloon came a blare of noise and up the street a second little saloon emitted the strains of a tiny piano.

A discreet light showed from behind the drawn shades of the Cattlemen's Association, also the office of Walt Ruebens, banker and agent to most of the big ranchers, whom Oscar Bragg used to say was a 'grabby chuck of blubber', a puppet for the big men.

Mason tried the door and found it unlocked. He pushed it open and entered, closing the door behind him. There was an inner door, and when he opened this the heat from the stove hit him. In a lamplit room were three men – Hank Bonnadeen, Rance Cash and the blubber-like Mr Ruebens.

'I am Lee Clay,' the man who had called himself Mason announced.

The three men were on their feet.

'We have been expecting you,' said Hank Bonnadeen and pushed a chair towards the visitor.

Clay ignored it. He said, 'I remember you, Bonnadeen. Who are these jaspers?'

'This is Rance Cash, of the Bar B, and Walt Ruebens – guess we don't need to keep you, Ruebens.'

The fat man gave an uneasy laugh.

'No secrets from me, I hope, Hank.'

Lee Clay stared at him with his ice-cold eyes.

'No secrets from anyone. You sent for a gun, Bonnadeen. I brought it.' He paused, then added deliberately, 'Who do you want me to kill?'

Walt Ruebens' face was suddenly gleaming, glistening with sweat. 'That's hard talk, mister.'

'Take it easy,' snapped Cash. 'Clay, we want to tie things up around here. Maybe you can help us out.'

The gunslinger shrugged, then slowly started to unbutton his sheepskin jacket.

'Mebbe I can, mebbe I can't.' He looked from one to the other, from the slim, taut Bonnadeen to the scowling face of Rance Cash and the frightened one of Ruebens, the agent. 'Get one thing straight, gents, I am not here to do nobody no favours.'

Bonnadeen said, 'I have told you what price we will pay.'

'Tell me again,' insisted Clay.

'One thousand dollars – when the job is done.'

A slow smile touched the plain, almost homely features of the gunslinger. 'Not after,' he said coldly. 'Now.'

Rance Cash moved forward.

'See here, Clay, you are in no position to throw your weight around.' Then he stopped, as if the coldness of the gunslinger's stare had frozen his words.

'You reckon not, mister?' Clay said.

His tone was deceptively mild, and Cash plunged on again: 'You are a wanted man, Clay – do I have to remind you? You rode with Cannon and there is still a price on your head?'

'Yep, ten thousand dollars to be precise,' nodded Lee Clay, 'dead or alive.' His tight smile. 'Makes you think, don't it, mister? A quick bullet and you have scored your-self ten thousand iron men. How about you, mister? You ready to risk your gun against mine?'

Walt Ruebens forced a laugh, but Bonnadeen said softly, 'There is always a bullet in the back, Clay.'

With a tiger-like spring, Lee Clay was on him, his move so swift that it shocked the others. Crowding Hank Bonnadeen against the wall, he said, 'Threats I don't like.' He pitched his voice higher. 'My back is to you now, gents. Start workin' on it – and Bonnadeen's a dead man!'

Almost magically his gun was in his hand, the muzzle rammed against the rancher's suddenly rigid belly. Rance Cash found his voice.

'Don't be a fool, Clay. We don't want your angry, mangy hide – nor the reward! We are rich men – rich enough to buy you and a dozen more like you – back off there!'

Clay sprang away from Bonnadeen, and the gun barrel danced in the lamplight, then it was gone, and he was brushing his fingertips together, smiling a little.

'You are so right, Mr Cash. You could buy a dozen men like me – but how many ready to take the risk? How many can you really count on?' His head jerked on his neck, taking in one man after the other. 'Sure there is a price on my head. They would put me where Cannon is tomorrow if they could catch me! I have always been that much too fast for them!'

'They nearly took you a couple of months back at Jackson Springs – I heard about that.' It was Ruebens sud-denly, finding his tongue.

'Sure I was at Jackson Springs, but they weren't any-where near to catchin' me,' Clay said calmly. 'I take it you were hiding out at Langford's place?'

'Not all the time, mister! Why, I even went to the pen, and they didn't spot me!' Clay said with pride.

'That's hard to swallow, Clay.'

'It is the truth! I went right in there with Letha Kent, John Cannon's gal. She said I was her brother come along to look out for her.' He laughed, throwing his head back, then cut the laugh off short. 'I went right into the pen and they took us into a room and then brought Cannon in. The guards stood all around the walls. I talked with John Cannon and he with me. I walked right outa that pen a free man. I tell you it is the truth, gents . . .' He leaned forward eagerly. 'Nobody spotted me – though a half dozen prisoners were there. They knew who I was, all right!' Again he laughed abruptly. 'Those guards must have been plenty sore when they heard that I had slipped through their fingers. They never got another chance to nail me.'

'It still doesn't alter the fact that you are a wanted man, and as such you have got to go mighty quietly,' Rance Cash added.

Lee Clay looked at Cash, who had spoken, then nodded.

'Sure enough does. But, by the same token, gents, you three can't afford to be too easy! Guess the law in this town would be plenty interested to know you sent for me – and to know a few other things beside!'

Hank Bonnadeen said thinly, 'And just what does that mean?'

'It means, mister, that you are in the same shape as I am, only – there is no price on your heads! That is the only difference, gents.'

Cash said, 'There is a world of difference between you and us, make no mistake, Clay.'

'And you make no mistake, either. How about if it got around that some of you gents tied in with John Cannon and his bunch in the high old days?' Clay laughed at the expressions on their faces, and then he taunted them. 'It don't do to remember those times, eh, gents? The gay old times when John Cannon rode up and down the mountain and took the cattle he chose! With your help, gents – it was always pretty useful to have the backing of some of you ranchers!'

The agent, Walt Ruebens, blurted out, 'It only happened once!'

'Once – twice – what is the real difference?'

Ruebens was silent, and Lee Clay went on, 'Awkward questions, gents – and I got the answers to 'em! Don't you forget that, none of you!'

'You are proving nothing, Clay,' said Cash.

Bonnadeen said frostily, 'We have hired you to come here, Clay – not to listen to you preach to us!'

'Preaching? Is that what I'm doin'? I could give the law a fine old bit of preachifyin' if I had a mind to! For instance, who killed Ben Flynn?'

'Seth Carver did it!'

'Carver? Sure, why not? But he was on your payroll, too, wasn't he, Bonnadeen? Flynn was on to your games – he warned you the game was up and that is why you had him killed,' Clay replied directly.

'That will be enough, Clay.'

'Enough and to spare,' nodded the gunslinger, his

mouth twisted bitterly. 'But don't you get high and mighty with me, Bonnadeen, or you others! How many of you are in it? It don't matter. The point is none of you can afford to get sassy with me, and don't you forget it!'

'All right,' Hank Bonnadeen said, 'you have had your say and made your point.'

'I will always have my say! I am not like old man Flynn – writin' everything down, puttin' it in some book – a fool thing to do. . . .'

'How's that?' Bonnadeen was starting forward suddenly.

Clay said, 'All I know I keep in my head. That is why I didn't get caught with Cannon and the rest of the boys. I got a headpiece – and I use it! I aim to get right on usin' it – my headpiece and my gun. There ain't no law in this whole West that can hold me.'

They had heard him out, although the three of them were strained and tense, thinking of what he had said before. It was Bonnadeen who spoke first. 'What do you know about Flynn and the book he wrote?'

'What don't I know about Flynn?' Lee Clay stared at Hank Bonnadeen and then the others, suddenly cagey.

'You knew he kept a record of all the cattle he lost and the comings and goings – all that that ranny spilled to him when Flynn caught him up on the north line that time. . . .'

'The man who was killed,' nodded Walt Ruebens.

'You had him killed, you ranchers,' taunted Clay, 'but – how come the big stares, gents? Are you tryin' to make me believe you didn't know about Ben Flynn keepin' a record? Langford knew—'

Cash said swiftly, 'Of course we knew – it is plain, isn't

it? Flynn was dangerous – and that is why he had to be silenced.'

'That is for the record, too,' sneered Clay. 'But say, Bonnadeen, you look sick. What is buzzin' in that brain of yours?' He paused. 'Let's have it, Hank. It is about Flynn and his records, huh?'

'Forget it,' Rance Cash said, but Lee Clay laughed.

'Why would I? I guess I landed onto somethin' here! Damned if it ain't just hit me! You gents killed Flynn before you got his book! How about if someone found that book? Have to do some more "silencing", wouldn't you?'

Bonnadeen wet his lips suddenly. Ruebens blundered in: 'Lena Flynn was at Sennett's office today – I saw her drive up. And – by thunder, I remember now! She lifted an old valise out of the rig and Sennett ran out and helped her with it. They carried it into his office—'

'Shut down,' snarled Cash and Ruebens mumbled to silence.

Clay, looking at them all with a grin on his face, said, 'Talk about a hornets' nest! But, say now, gents – you don't have to look so sick, all of you! You are in trouble, so you sent for me. Who is my gun for?' His grin suddenly went. 'Not the gal? The Flynn gal?'

'No, no!'

Lee Clay said sourly, 'It better not be! I don't hire out my gun to cut down no whey-faced gal! Set a man against me – give me a target, gents! Who is it that has crossed you up?'

'His name is Luke Bragg,' said Bonnadeen deliberately. His words seemed to hum in the air, after he had uttered them. Then the silence was shattered by Clay's laugh.

'Luke Bragg? The man who killed George York?'

'You know him?' Bonnadeen asked, surprised.

'Know him? Sure, sure! That is, I seen him once – at the pen that time in Jackson Springs where I called on John Cannon with Letha Kent. There had been a lotta talk about Luke Bragg. He was fast and mean – he cut that mangy gambler down like he was made of soapstone! Yeah, sure, I seen him – and talked with him for a minute, too!'

'That is interesting,' said Hank Bonnadeen flatly, and he and Rance Cash exchanged glances.

Walt Ruebens said, 'If you know him, then it will make it easier. He has got to be removed, Mr Clay.'

'Then you remove him,' said Clay contemptuously, and started to button up his jacket.

Bonnadeen said sharply, 'Let's have no misunderstanding about this, Clay. Get Bragg out of the way and we will pay you a thousand dollars.'

'You will pay me now,' Lee Clay replied coldly.

'Half now and half when the job is finished.'

Lee Clay shrugged, said nothing either way.

Hank Bonnadeen held out a hand to Reubens, twitching his fingers impatiently. Ruebens slowly extracted a folded wad of bills from an inner pocket and handed them over. These Bonnadeen leafed through rapidly, then passed them to Clay. For a moment it seemed as though Clay wouldn't take the bills, then with another shrug he flicked them from Bonnadeen's hand and stuffed them away.

'How about Mick Gardner?' he asked.

Rance Cash answered, 'You owe Gardner plenty. It is up to you to deal with him.'

'We want him wiped out, too,' Bonnadeen said flatly.

Clay exclaimed, 'You aimin' to tangle with Gardner?' There was incredulity in his voice.

Hank said, 'He has run against us. It is time he went.'

'It will be my pleasure,' said Clay, and lightly dusted his fingers together. 'Give me twenty-four hours.'

'Make it fast as you can,' said Bonnadeen. There was anxiety in his voice. 'Bragg's fast. Did you know that? He has already killed two men – including Seth Carver.'

'You don't say!' grinned Clay, and stood thinking for a moment. Then suddenly, 'He had a big rep down in Jackson Springs. A hard man with a gun . . . where do I find him?'

'Right at this moment,' replied Bonnadeen, 'he is at the Johnson House where he booked a room. He has taken over the spread at Black Hills, but right now he is in town. You want to take him, Clay, you will have to move fast . . . and town would be the best place.'

'You tryin' to teach me my trade, Hank?' Lee Clay was grinning mirthlessly. 'Well, gents, it has been a pleasure.' The gunslinger gave an iconic bow, turned and went out into the night.

After he was gone, a heavy silence hung in the room. Ruebens broke it by saying ruefully, 'I don't like the look of all of this – not one bit!'

Hank Bonnadeen said harshly, 'There was no call for you to stay, Ruebens!'

'I am in it as deep as you are,' said the agent resentfully.

'Why try to keep me out? I have got as much to lose as you two do.'

'Don't talk like a fool!' snarled Bonnadeen. 'Cash and I are the only losers if the Flynn affair ever gets out! Or if Luke Bragg's left to rampage around this valley ruining all we have built up! Rance and I – and a couple of others who don't count anyway.'

'You sure like to make me feel small, Bonnadeen,' said the fat man resentfully. 'If it hadn't been for me you would never have got onto Langford. And where would you have been without John Cannon?'

'It would have been better for us if we would have never known John Cannon and his bunch,' said Hank, and Rance Cash nodded soberly. Of the three of them Cash was the calmest. Solid, sure of himself, he was tougher than Bonnadeen, and certainly tougher than the pudgy agent who moved across the room, took his hat off the peg, and started for the door.

'Where in hell do you think you are going now, Ruebens?' snapped Hank Bonnadeen, and the fat man turned heavily.

'I don't stay around where I am not wanted,' Reubens fired back.

'You stayed long enough to hear what Lee Clay had to say!'

'What harm is in that?' demanded Ruebens. 'Figure I can't be trusted? After all, like you said, I have got nothing to gain or lose – either way.'

'There is the reward on Clay,' said Rance Cash, and Walt Ruebens smiled slowly.

'Yes,' he replied, 'ten thousand dollars . . . that is a lot of money, gents. I will give you both good evening.'

Lena Flynn had not returned to the Sunrise spread after her interview with Tim Sennett. She felt she had to know what transpired between Sennett and the sheriff, and decided at last to stay in town till she could get the chance to have further words with the lawyer. She had one friend in town – the daughter of the mayor, Martha Allin, a girl of her own age, and just about the only woman around Preston Gulch with whom Lena had much in common. So she went to the Allins' house and stayed there until, becoming restless again, she went back into town and called at Sennett's office. She found the place locked up and could get no news of the lawyer. Making her way uncertainly down the street, she ran into Luke Bragg.

In the lamplight spilling from Pringle's store, Bragg recognized her instantly, stopped and said, 'This is a late hour for you to be walking around.'

Recognition had been immediate with her as well. She was angry with herself to find her heart beating a little faster, and her voice was uneven as she replied, 'I feel it is none of your business, Mr Bragg, where or when I am out.'

When he said nothing more, she went on impatiently, 'It isn't very late at that, and it so happens I have been looking for an old friend.'

'I hope you found him, ma'am,' Bragg offered back.

'I didn't – if you must know.'

'If it was Sheriff Gardner you were looking for—'

'I wasn't looking for him.' She paused, adding, 'It was Tim Sennett.'

'The lawyer? Maybe he is with Gardner, too, round at

132

the Palace Saloon.'

'You sound very sure. But I suppose you spend a lot of time in saloons and such places,' she said.

'I was there. In the back room,' nodded Bragg, tall and somehow menacing in the half light. 'The truth is the man who works for me at Black Hills, old Tramp Eckelmann, ran into a little trouble.'

'Rufus? I guess he is often in trouble—'

'Not this kind of trouble! Seems he hit town and went to the saloon. Wilson Cameron was there liquoring up. Drowning his sorrows. Cameron talked up a lot against Hank Bonnadeen and the other big ranchers. There were cowpokes there and they resented it. There was a fight and Cameron broke a few heads before they subdued him. In the fracas, old Tramp drew cards,' explained Bragg. There was a faint thread of amusement in his voice. 'Maybe he reckoned he had to take the part of the sheepman. At all events, as he left the saloon he was gun whipped.'

The girl gave a little gasp.

'The poor old man! Who would do such a thing like that?'

'You don't have to guess too hard to get the answer to that one,' Bragg quipped.

'You mean—?'

'The ranchers are playing it hard. These cowpokes . . . they are paid hands, and they are ignorant men at best. They take their lead from Bonnadeen and the other ranchers. At all events, someone made sure of getting Rufus Eckelmann as he stepped out into the darkness. He is lucky to be alive,' Bragg replied.

In a low voice the woman said, 'This is terrible, Mr

Bragg. Just terrible.'

'You might call it a skirmish in the range war. That is all.'

'People have got hurt – skirmish or not, Mr Bragg. Why don't you end it?' she asked.

'Me?' Bragg gave a short laugh. 'I didn't start this war, Miss Lena.'

She nodded. 'But you could end it!'

'Could I? You tell me how to do it and I will consider it,' Luke Bragg said.

'Make a truce with the ranchers – surely you could come to terms—'

'A man can't come to terms with a nest of rattlesnakes. And besides – the townsmen of Preston Gulch are taking the war into their own hands now. A whole lot of men liked the way Cameron was talking up – they were sorry for him – and bitter about his son being killed. When the fight started, the cowpokes were outnumbered ten to one. After they brought Rufus indoors, blood all over his head, the townsmen's anger really broke out. So you see, ma'am, right now the sheriff's hands are plenty full. And maybe your friend Sennett's as well,' Bragg explained.

'Yet you aren't there where the trouble is?' she asked coyly.

'The trouble's over right now. But it could break out afresh any time. I am heading back to the hotel to get my gear. I am pulling up stakes.'

'Leaving town, Mr Bragg?' the woman asked.

'Getting ready to move any place,' he told her gravely and stood aside to let her pass.

Lena hesitated for a moment, and then moved forward.

For an instant their bodies brushed against each other. He heard her quick intake of breath, then she was gone into the shadows of the night.

CHAPTER 11

Luke Bragg threw open the door of his hotel room and stopped short. A man was sitting in the chair inside his room. He was grinning, which made Bragg very uneasy.

'Please come right in, Bragg! Come right in!'

For a moment Bragg didn't recognize his caller. Then, as the other man moved, the lamplight fell squarely across his face, and Bragg, with a grunt, threw himself sideways, heeling back the door as he did so. It closed with a crack like a pistol shot, but the man in the chair made no move to draw his gun. He sat very still under the menace of Luke Bragg's drawn gun.

'No call for that, mister.' The man got to his feet, taking his time. 'You know me – I am Clay, only in this town they call me Mason.'

Luke Bragg nodded slowly and gestured with his gun. 'Turn around,' he said, 'and I will have your hardware.'

'Is that any way to treat an old friend?' protested the gunslinger, then grinned. 'Say now, put away that shootin' iron. There won't be any need for gun play between the two of us.'

'I remember seeing you,' said Bragg, 'back there in the Jackson Springs pen. The day you visited with John Cannon, the cattle thief. After you had gone there was a lot of talk about you, and the boys were plenty happy over you treating the guards like that.'

'Glad you remembered me,' said Lee Clay affably. 'But you didn't have a bad reputation yourself. And that is why I am here, Bragg.'

'Just why?'

'Bragg, I got the hotel clerk to open this room – no trouble at all! I got a headpiece and a gun. I use both!' He paused, but Luke Bragg stood like a statue, the gun jutting from his side. 'I got into this room – your room - and I could have blasted you the moment you opened the door. But I didn't. Wonderin' why, Bragg?'

'Why don't you just tell me why?'

'And I am tellin' you. I came here to kill you,' Clay said simply.

'I figured it might have been something like that,' Bragg replied.

'But when I had the chance I didn't take it. On account I would rather have you alive.'

'Keep talking,' said Bragg.

'Just to show you I mean well, Bragg.' He dropped his hand to the buckle of his gun belt and while Bragg kept him covered, undid it and let it fall to the floor. 'How about that, Bragg? Is it a truce?'

By way of answering, Luke Bragg strode over to him, and with his free hand rapidly slapped him around, looking for a hidden gun. He found none.

'I am clean, Bragg,' noted Clay.

Luke Bragg stepped back, holstered his gun, folded his arms across his chest and waited.

Clay said, 'I will make a deal with you. Ride along with me and I will split with you.'

'Split what?'

'Bragg, you know what they are payin' me to kill you?' He waited, but Bragg said nothing. 'One thousand dollars. I have half of it on me already.' Clay laughed. 'Do I have to tell you the names of these gents who are so free with their money?'

'Bet I can guess them.'

'Start guessin', Bragg, and see how close you are,' Clay said with a snicker.

'I have been close ever since I have been in this valley,' retorted Luke Bragg. 'I have been right in the middle of a range war – a war I didn't start.'

'So I hear tell. But what made you tangle with a big hombre like Bonnadeen? And that other one – Rance Cash?'

'Of the Crazy 8?' nodded Bragg. 'They are the two ring-leaders.'

'There is another man,' added Clay, as if eager to show his goodwill. 'He is fat, and don't look like a rancher – I think they call him Ruebens.' Again the gunslinger paused, but Luke Bragg only stared at him. 'It all adds up to this. They are ready to pay a thousand dollars just to get you out of the way. And Gardner, too. But that is my own grudge fight, I reckon. Now I am in Preston Gulch I might as well even up the old score . . . you get my drift, Bragg?'

'I am getting nothing as yet.'

'You soon will!' Lee Clay moved closer to the other

man. 'These ranchers have been riding high and hand-some for a long time. They are plenty rich and they reckon that is enough. There could be enough for us – if we played it right.'

Bragg shot him a look. 'Meaning?'

'We have got enough on Bonnadeen and Cash to send them both to the pen for fifty years or so! But we don't want them there. What use would they be to us?' He grinned at Bragg. 'All we have to do is ask 'em real nice – and mebbe prod 'em around a little – and they will pay. Man, they will pay but good!'

'Blackmail,' nodded Luke Bragg.

The other said instantly, 'Why not? It is as good a word as any. Mind, we have to make a quick killin'. I don't believe in comin' right out in the open and movin' around free and easy so any gun toter from one of the big spreads can cut us down from an alley! We move in on Bonnadeen and Cash tonight – make 'em pay up by noon tomorrow and then get out. What do you say, Bragg?'

'What sum did you have in mind?' Bragg asked.

'To get from them? I would say a hundred thousand.'

'Dollars?' Luke Bragg sounded genuinely startled.

'I don't mean Spanish pesetas, friend! One hundred thousand dollars should be a nice enough price for our silence and – say, I just got another idea,' Clay replied.

'Yeah?'

'That business about Ben Flynn getting killed. You know they were back of it?'

'I had guessed.'

'Sure,' nodded Clay. 'But tonight I sprang somethin' on them – they didn't know that Flynn kept a record – a diary or some such nonsense. Langford told me of it back in Jackson Springs. You know something? We could get a hold of that diary and it would be worth another hundred thousand! There is nothing like havin' things written down in black and white – clean proof that these ranchers were runnin' with John Cannon's bunch; they were in as deep as any of us owl hoots! And there is the gal – Ben Flynn's daughter – they spoke of her tonight too.'

'They did, eh?' Bragg's tone was hard as steel, but Clay seemed not to notice, went right on.

'Mebbe we could make a bigger killin' than we think. We got Cash and Bonnadeen right where we want them! Now – what do you say, Bragg? You comin' in with me?'

'I am wondering why you would want me,' Bragg said.

'A fair question,' nodded Clay. 'Like I always say, I use my headpiece. I could have killed you tonight – but that ain't the way I like to work my trade. I never was an ambusher! What is more, I reckon I need a jasper like you, Bragg. You are smart, I heard all about you back in Jackson Springs. You are fast, you are clever and – together we could clean up a half million if we have a mind to!'

Luke Bragg said calmly, 'You have got it all wrong, Clay. I am not against the law.'

'Against it or for it, what is the difference? They jailed you, didn't they?'

'For a killing I had done,' answered Bragg.

'York had it coming – I know all about it! But they still made you sweat it out, with the rats and the roaches waitin' for a stacked trial! You were lucky you wasn't hung, you know that, Bragg?' said Lee Clay.

Bragg nodded. 'I know it.'

'Well, then! Why should you worry which side you are on? I tell you, we can get rich, go where we like, do what we like, doesn't that sound nice?'

'It won't wash, Clay. I came up here to take over a ranch I inherited from my uncle. I have got that place and I aim to stick it out,' he paused. 'I owe my uncle that much.'

'Then you are a fool,' snapped Clay cheerfully. 'Why be a rancher when you can lord it in Mexico with a dozen pretty *señoritas* and a six-inch stogie in your face? It don't make any sense.'

'Maybe it doesn't to you, but that is the way I am made and that is the way I will play it,' explained Bragg.

'Then it looks like I will have to kill you,' Clay replied coolly.

'Yeah,' said Bragg, 'you will if you want to push your ideas.'

'Meanin' you would try to stop me?' asked Clay.

'I would have to,' offered Luke Bragg.

'Aimin' to take the side of those polecats, Bonnadeen and Cash?'

Luke Bragg shook his head. 'I am not taking any side but my own. I have had those cattle ranchers against me right through, and I am taking over where my uncle left off. What is more, a good man died because of them, and maybe I am taking up the fight for him.'

'Flynn,' nodded Clay. 'Well, that is fine and noble but it won't get you no place. I tell you, Bragg, I can't afford to have your cross my trail. It will have to be you or me.'

'In that case,' said Bragg, 'we will cut it short.' He unfolded his arms. 'I am taking you in, Clay.'

'For the reward?' asked the gunslinger.

141

'The hell with that! Like you said, it is you or me. I have got a gun, you haven't. It is too bad but . . . you called the play,' Bragg reasoned.

'You are right!' said Clay. 'Dead right. And I am sweatin' for it!' He plucked off his hat and wiped his forehead with the sleeve of his jacket.

Luke Bragg said, 'Kick your gun belt my way, Clay, just so you don't get tempted. Remember, I don't want to have to kill you.'

'Before you kill me you have got to have your gun workin', friend!' Clay said.

He was holding his hat in his left hand. His right hand suddenly darted inside the hat and came out with a stubby derringer. Bragg heard the click of the tiny hammer as it went back.

'Always I use my headpiece,' said Lee Clay cheerfully. 'I never leave nothin' to chance, and I am always ready for the next move – even if it is to kingdom come! You had best reach high, Bragg, else I will have to put a little slug plumb through your head.'

Impassively, Luke Bragg raised his hands. Clay stepped lightly up to him.

'I am givin' you a last chance. Mebbe I am loco, but hell, I like the looks of you! You are different from them mangy polecats, them no-good ranchers! You are a fighter and you have lived hard. Same as me. There is no difference between you and me.'

'Except that I live by something and you have forgotten what it was,' said Bragg.

'You goin' to preach me a sermon, Bragg? I don't need that,' spat Clay.

'Then kill me and be done with it!'

Lee Clay laughed, stepped back and snatched up his gun belt. He circled Luke Bragg, made for the door. 'Turn around before I close the door and you are real dead!'

Bragg called out in surprise, 'You are the loco one, Clay, letting me live. Unless you aim to quit – leave town.'

'I ain't leaving, Bragg, but like I told you, I ain't no bushwhacker neither. Cross me and I will kill you, but get real smart and go out to that mangy ranch of yours and live to a ripe old age. Or join me. What do you say, Bragg?'

'Just close the door and go out,' said Luke Bragg without turning, though his pulses were thudding and he could feel the sweat on his palms. He heard Clay swear under his breath. Then there was a brief pause and the door opened and closed, not loudly, but firmly.

Luke Bragg's body relaxed. It was his turn to mop his brow with his sleeve. Then he took out his six gun and checked it carefully. For the first time in his life he knew that he was up against no ordinary gunslinger. Clay was a man who talked a lot, yet who backed up his talk and would stop at nothing. Just nothing. He turned down the lamp.

CHAPTER 12

Tim Sennett had reached the door of his Main Street office when he felt something hard pressed into the small of his back, and a voice from the darkness said,

'Open that door and be mighty quick about it.'

Sennett's first reaction was to face his attacker. But the hard object – which he assumed was a gun – bored into his spine and the voice came again: 'This gun means business, Sennett.'

'Hank!' exclaimed the lawyer.

The voice said, 'Open the damn door and get inside! Make a sound and I will blow your spine out!'

Trembling a little, Sennett unlocked the door, pushed it open. As he moved into the room he heard the door close behind him. He started to turn but Bonnadeen said, 'Keep right on going and if you know what is good for you, you will do as I say and nothing foolish.'

Sennett went through to his inner office. A lamp was burning on his desk, turned down. As he turned up the wick he cast desperately around in his mind for some means of overpowering the rancher. He remembered the gun in the top drawer of his desk. But it was around the other side.

Bonnadeen's voice broke sharply across his frantic thoughts. 'You look after Ben Flynn's affairs. Where are his papers?'

Tim Sennett swung around to face him in sudden awareness and, with it, blind panic surged through him. He gasped out, 'What do you want with those papers, Bonnadeen?' But even as he spoke, he knew. The rancher was smiling faintly.

'I am taking those papers, Sennett. Everything that Flynn wrote about his cattle losses and the rest, I believe you know what I am talking about.'

Sennett, in an attempt at bluster, said, 'All I know is that you have forced your way in here at gunpoint – you, one of the biggest figures in the valley! It is hard to believe that a man of your stature – of all people—'

'Save your breath,' Bonnadeen broke in. 'This is the showdown. I know that you have the records. I want them now!'

'I have nothing here.'

'Don't make me force you to do as I ask.' Bonnadeen took a step closer, but Sennett faced him without a tremor. 'I am not alone in this, Sennett. Cash is out there – the others besides, if I need them. This is our town, Sennett, and things are going to be done our way from this time on, understand?'

Tim Sennett sniffed. 'Does the law count for nothing anymore?'

'It won't after tonight.'

'You can't be planning to get rid of Sheriff Gardner!'

'Why not?' Bonnadeen's tone was cool. Now the chips were down, he was as remorseless as Clay had ever been. 'Time has run out for you, Sennett. Produce those papers – and be quick about it!'

'You might as well just kill me then, Hank, and be done with it. I am giving you nothing.'

Bonnadeen raised the gun and struck. Sennett fell back against the desk, blood streaming from the cut in his cheek. Through white lips he said, 'It is no use, Hank. Kill me and you will still find nothing here.'

With a curse, the rancher glanced swiftly about him. His eyes lighted on the iron safe in the corner of the office.

'Keys!' he demanded, and held out an impatient left hand.

Tim Sennett stared back at him, still arched over the desk, the blood trickling down his face and pooling on the desk.

'You asked for it, Sennett,' snarled Bonnadeen, and struck again, only this time the lawyer was ready for him and rolled with the blow, which caught him on the top of the shoulder. He crashed down, and Bonnadeen fell on top of him, grunting as he rained blows on the other man's head with the gun butt. Sennett made a desperate grab, clutched the rancher, hauled himself up and lashed out with both fists. But years of heavy drinking had drained him of his strength. He was helpless against Bonnadeen's ferocity. Once more he fell, and this time Bonnadeen crashed a boot into the side of his head. The lawyer lay still.

Bonnadeen took time out to get his breath, then, sliding his gun back inside his coat, he stooped, swiftly searched Sennett and found his keys. He tore them loose from the chain, hurried over to the safe and tried key after key until he found the right one. As he swung back the heavy door, he glanced back at the lawyer, who hadn't moved.

It didn't take Bonnadeen long to find the great pile of books which held Ben Flynn's records. He carried the topmost one over to the table, flipped it open under the lamp. He read a few lines, then with a grunt of satisfaction went back to the safe to get the rest out. He had his back turned to the desk when Sennett got first to his knees, then, by using the desk for support, onto to his feet. He swayed for a moment and then snatched open the desk drawer and plucked out the pistol.

Hank Bonnadeen turned in that instant. For a moment he stared, slack jawed, then with an oath, he dropped his burden and dove for his gun. Despairingly, Sennett tried to fire his gun. The hammer went back at last, but it was too late. Bonnadeen punched a vicious shot from across the room and the lawyer was thrown back, sprawling, losing off his gun as he fell to the floor.

Bonnadeen stood crouched for a few moments, staring through a wreath of gun smoke at the fallen man. There came a shout from outside, and with a quick surge of panic he slid the gun out of sight and ran for the door. His first thought was escape – escape from the results of his crime, the damning evidence of Ben Flynn's diaries. He had to find Rance Cash . . . He plucked open the door. The cold struck him fiercely, and footsteps on the iron-hard boardwalk rang as townsmen came running, drawn by the sound of the gun shots. For an instant, Hank

Bonnadeen hesitated, then dove out onto the street, melted into the shadows before he could be seen. As he rounded the corner of the building he came up hard against a bulky figure.

A growling curse and then, 'Rance! Thank heaven it's you—'

'What in hell has been going on, Hank?' Cash asked.

'Sennett got ornery – and . . .'

The other rancher stared at Bonnadeen. 'You killed him?'

'I guess I did. But, Rance, there are papers – records – a whole pile of books that . . .'

'We have got to get to them before anyone sees them!'

'But there are people out front there – just take a look!'

Bonnadeen's voice was weakened from his fight and escape.

Rance Cash stood for a moment in sullen silence and then, 'What is wrong with a little fire?'

'Fire?' said a frantic Bonnadeen.

'Why not? You got matches on you, right?' asked Cash.

'I guess so.' Hank Bonnadeen fumbled inside his jacket.

'Better still – that carbide lamp! Get it!' ordered Rance Cash.

Without a word, Bonnadeen turned and plunged across to the corner, reached up and hauled down one of the flaring lamps that hung there. He ran back with it. Rance Cash called out sharply, 'Don't fool around with it. Use that window!'

Teeth bared, hair streaming, Bonnadeen looked like a madman as he hurled the lamp through the glass of the side window. Then he jumped back as flame spouted. 'Let Sennett fry!' he gasped, and Cash grabbed him by the arm.

'If we are seen around here, we are as good as dead!'

'What do I care now?' There was a note of almost crazy triumph in Bonnadeen's voice. 'Once those records are destroyed – we are clear!'

'There is still the Flynn woman,' warned Cash, as they hurried down the back lane that speared off from Main Street. Bonnadeen stopped short at that, then, with another laugh, hurried on.

Rance Cash called after him, 'What is with you? Where do you think you are going?'

Hank Bonnadeen made no reply, but disappeared into the darkness. Cash, with an angry shrug, turned away, headed back towards Main. Like Bonnadeen, he was obsessed, but not with the desire to wipe out all the records of the rustlers' activities on Sunrise. He was remembering that Clay was in town, and that Clay had been paid to get Bragg – and the sheriff, too. Mick Gardner was the man Cash feared the most, even more than Bragg, for Gardner represented the law. He was the man who brought in John Cannon, in spite of all his guns. Gardner wore the badge. He was the symbol.

He had to go.

Sheriff Mick Gardner had not heard the shots from Sennett's office. At that time, he was in the law office with tintypes spread out on the table in the lamplight.

'Recognize any of these, Ruebens?'

The fat agent scarcely glanced at the smudged likenesses on the desktop. 'I tell you, it is Clay, the gunslinger! He is here in town and he is out to get Luke Bragg!'

'So you said, but – would this be the man?' asked the sheriff.

Ruebens stared at the tintype Gardner had thrust to one side and shook his head vigorously. 'No, not that one! There is the man!' His shaking finger was jabbed at another of the likenesses and Gardner looked up sharply.

'That is Lee Clay, sure enough! John Cannon's top gun – the most wanted of all of his gang,' the sheriff conceded.

'And there is a big reward out on him, isn't there, Sheriff?' Ruebens was suddenly ingratiating; he even tried to smile. 'For turning him in, I am entitled to that reward, aren't I?'

Mick Gardner regarded him with disfavour, then said, 'You will be entitled to some of it, I reckon.' He reached for a spare gun and thrust it into the waistband of his pants. 'Where shall I find this man?'

'I told you! He went round to the hotel to find Luke Bragg. The ranchers paid him to come here and kill Bragg. And he said he was out to get you too, Sheriff!'

As if he hadn't heard, Mick Gardner moved lazily back to the desk, proceeded to turn down the wick of the lamp. Ruebens cried impatiently, 'Hurry it up, can't you, Sheriff? He might get away!'

Gardner stared at the big man, a faint smile on his face.

'Before he is done his work? Don't worry, Ruebens, he will be around. Let's go, shall we?'

Ruebens drew back. 'You are not asking me to go out on Main Street, are you, Sheriff?'

'I wasn't asking; I was telling you.'

Ruebens quavered, 'But if the ranchers see me with you, they – they might get the wrong idea. . . .'

'Now wouldn't that be too bad? Come on, Ruebens. I want you out there,' insisted the sheriff.

Still the fat man made no move. Gardner grabbed him roughly by the arm, and thrust him towards the door. 'It is tough being an informer. You startin' to find that out?'

From the cell in the back came the sound of Clint Murdoch's jeering laugh. Both the sheriff and the agent had forgotten about the Crazy 8 puncher who had been hanging on the bars, drinking in every word he could hear from the inner office.

'So they sent a gun to get you, Sheriff?' he jeered. 'Now, ain't that too bad! You and Luke Bragg – that Lee Clay is plenty fast I hear! You will need all your artillery, Gardner! All you have got – and more! And how about it, Ruebens? Ain't you scared too?'

'Save your breath, Murdoch,' Gardner said. 'You will need it when that rope tightens round your throat.'

He opened the door, turning up the fur collar of his jacket as he did so. Then, as he started down the board-walk, he raised his head sharply. Behind him Ruebens was shivering.

'There is trouble – all the folks are running. . . .'

'Fire at Tim Sennett's place!' shouted the sheriff and, arms swinging, set off down the street, Ruebens a few paces behind, hugging the shadows, head down.

They came to the scene of the fire, and had to push their way through the crowd, which was increasing every minute.

Then a voice called out, 'Here he comes!'

Ruebens blurted out, 'Someone's coming – out of the building!'

The sheriff started forward. The man he thrust aside turned with an oath, then, recognizing the sheriff, said, 'How about that, Sheriff? Someone said Sennett was in there – he was seen through the window! And that jasper from Black Hills busted right in and – look there, Sheriff! He has got him, all right!' It was Luke Bragg, standing outlined at the old frame building behind him. In his arms he carried the limp body of Tim Sennett. As the sheriff started forward, Bragg swung away from the building, handed over Sennett's body, a dozen willing hands to help him appeared.

'Been busy, Bragg?'

Bragg turned a blackened face and grinned, 'Heard about a gent down in San Francisco one time who got a medal for fighting a fire. How do I rate, Sheriff?'

'You need a drink?' the sheriff asked.

'I guess that can wait.' Luke Bragg stared about him eagerly, almost hungrily, and Gardner could feel new life pulsing from him. 'I got the lawyer out all right – and he is still alive. He had been shot and beaten up, by the look of him. What's more, Sheriff, I found the inside office shambled up plenty. Papers everywhere – big books like ledgers scattered around and everything burning like it was a barbecue. Sheriff, someone shot Sennett and put a torch to his office – to hide something . . . I reckon.'

'I guess that far,' said Mick Gardner tersely. He had all but forgotten the shivering person of Ruebens, who was sticking like a leech, scared almost to look behind him in case he should find an enemy there.

Gardner went on, 'Bonnadeen and Cash are behind all of this deviltry in this town, Bragg. I got the story now – just the details need to be filled in.'

'Details like Lee Clay, for instance?'

'You know about him?' the sheriff said, surprised.

'I talked with him tonight,' Bragg replied. 'Not by choice.'

They were starting to get water on the flames, forming a bucket chain from the hand pump in someone's backyard, ten lots down from the lawyer's office. But it was a futile gesture at best. The outer frame walls had caught now, and were burning fiercely. The crowd moved reluctantly back, licked by the yellow red glare, welcoming the excitement and the heat of it on such a bitter night. As Bragg moved away, the sheriff turned sharply as he felt a plucking at his sleeve. It was the agent – Ruebens – his face ghastly in the leaping light. 'Well, what is it?'

'He is there, Sheriff – there!'

'If you mean Bragg, he has gone to see how Sennett is.'

'No, not him, no . . . it is Clay!'

Mick Gardner saw him then; a slim, nondescript figure moving lightly around the fringe of the crowd. He seemed to be walking aimlessly, yet suddenly like quicksilver flicked by an impatient finger, his body leaped into action. A man and a woman were closest to him. He thrust at them, and they staggered to one side. The woman screamed shrilly, then, the man shouted a warning. The crowd swayed, then, started to scatter back.

'There he goes!' shouted Ruebens, and then ran off.

Clay laughed and cut Ruebens down, and laughed again.

153

'Come on and get me, Sheriff,' he crowed, and then was gone like a wraith, beyond the leaping ring of flames.

Mick Gardner was alone and yet the town crowded about him. He moved lightly forward, gun in his hand. Then from behind him a figure came bustling. It was Rance Cash, treading contemptuously over the ruptured bladder that had once been Ruebens. Coming right up to the sheriff, he cried, 'It is all right, Mick! I got him covered!'

With a snarled curse, Gardner tried to sidestep Cash's bulky figure. He managed to rap out, 'Keep clear, damn you! Keep clear of—'

It was too late. Rance Cash crowded right into him, spoiling his aim, throwing him to one side. And in that instant Clay snapped a shot from twenty feet away, fired, and laughed to see Gardner spin to one side, right hand stiffly raised, gun poking skywards.

'Nice work, Mr Rancher!' Clay was mincing forward now, probing for the kill. Mick Gardner lay helpless before him, the victim waiting for the sword.

And then Rance Cash's voice came, cracking with panic, 'Watch it, Clay! Just you watch it. . . !'

Luke Bragg had broken clear of the group around Tim Sennett at the corner of the alley. He didn't seem to be hurrying yet he covered the ground fast. Then he paused. His hand moved and the firelight winked briefly on blued steel, and then the gun roared, and as if at a signal Rance Cash collapsed slowly, his body crashing over the form of the sheriff.

'Not you, Bragg! I don't have to kill you, do I?'

Uncaring, Luke Bragg was moving again, but now he

was in range. The crowd was behind him, and spilled to one side, caught in shocked suspense, facing the dying flames from the burnt-out shell of Tim Sennett's office, watching death take the last few steps.

Lee Clay was gunning.

Drum fire rolled between the two men, full orchestra against the backdrop of the flames. Now Luke Bragg was face down, arms embracing the frozen street. A shuddering gasp ran through the crowd, but Clay, the gun, was on his knees as if praying, and now his right hand was empty. The drum fire had ceased; the orchestra stilled.

Luke Bragg was on one knee; across it his right forearm lay and his hand cradled the hot gun.

'Don't ... waste it ...' gasped Lee Clay, and tried to laugh, but choked on it at the last, and so died, still kneeling for an instant, then toppling over in a heap face down in the dirt.

Luke Bragg got to his feet and fresh blood gushed from the wound in his side. Stiffly he walked over to where Clay lay, and stared down at him. He spoke no word but he thought: *Now, there was a strange sort of man.*

And then the people of Preston Gulch were thronging and he was going back to where Mick Gardner lay. They tore Rance Cash's body off Mick Gardner, and raised him up.

'He is alive!'

'They don't die that easy,' said Luke Bragg, with a stiff smile as he looked into the clouded eyes of the sheriff.

Mick Gardner mumbled, 'Get these fools off me. I am but scratched. ...'

CHAPTER 13

He stood in the doorway of the parlour at the mayor's house, a thin, wild figure, with hair on end and fine clothes dishevelled. He was no longer Hank Bonnadeen, the smooth, well-educated rancher. He was a complete stranger, a foreign man with a gun in his hand and obscenities the like he had rarely – if ever – heard coming from his mouth.

'You will tell me how much you know, and how much you have told others! You will tell me quick, or by hell I—'

'Spare me your filthy, ridiculous threats,' said Lena Flynn, fighting to keep her voice steady and hide her fear. Back of her, beyond the half open door leading to the inner room, she knew the mayor and his wife and daughter were huddled, helpless before the hurricane that had raged into the house but a few minutes before in the form of Hank Bonnadeen. The rancher had his gun on Lena, and the woman knew, and Martha Allin knew, that if they dared make a move against him, Lena would die most assuredly.

'I am giving you ten seconds to speak,' mouthed Bonnadeen, then raised his voice to a shout. 'Speak, damn you! You—!'

'I will tell you whatever you want to know,' Lena replied, her head high. 'Then you will kill me, and after that they will kill you, Mr Bonnadeen!'

'Why, damn you—'

'Of course I know all about your dealings with John Cannon, and how my father found out, and died because of his knowledge! You think I am going to keep information like that to myself? Then you are a greater fool than I always thought you were,' she cried out.

'I killed Sennett!' screamed Bonnadeen, and he saw the woman blanch. 'I killed Sennett and I will kill you, too, and anybody else in this town who crosses me! I am Hank Bonnadeen and I am—'

'And you are dead!' said a voice from behind him.

Wilson Cameron had come in lightly for all his age and bulk, as if he knew this was his moment, and although the liquor had died in him he was driven by a hatred and something more; as if he had made himself into the avenger for the town, the sheepherders and, especially, his son.

'I followed you all the way up here from town, Bonnadeen. I followed along in the shadows. You didn't know I was there – but I only had to listen apiece out there to hear what you were at with Miss Lena here. Now I am here to square all accounts,' the man said.

Hank Bonnadeen was shaking with great fear, but he

never took his eyes off the wide-eyed woman. He screamed out, 'Kill me, and I will kill her!'

'That won't be much of a help to you, will it?'

'Then I will make a deal with you!' assured Bonnadeen.

'What sort of deal, Hank?' he paused. 'Will you agree to bring my boy back to life? Will you agree to give back my sheep you had killed? Will you agree to let me live peaceable, the way I had always done until you ranchers cut loose? Will you, Bonnadeen?'

Then Hank Bonnadeen moved. He jumped forward and grabbed Lena and dragged her body against his, swung her about like a shield between him and Cameron's gun. But Wilson Cameron was ready. He fired, and the bullet speared past Lena Flynn's flinching body, and spent itself inside Hank Bonnadeen. With a gurgling scream, the rancher staggered away like a drunken man, weaving and retching.

'You are finished, Bonnadeen,' said Wilson Cameron, looming like the avenger he felt himself to be. Then he shot Hank Bonnadeen in the mouth, amid the screams from Lena Flynn.

Luke Bragg and Tramp Eckelmann were putting up a chute at the end of the sheep corral by the Black Hills ranch house. At least, they were trying to build a chute. After an hour of it, Tramp threw down his end of the pole, swore loudly, and straightened and said, 'I ain't no use, Luke. My head is still spinnin' and look it here! Durned if you ain't started that bleeding again.'

Luke Bragg straightened, glanced down at his wounded side, and had to agree with Tramp.

'We will quit for a spell, old timer. Go indoors and start the coffee boiling.'

Tramp smiled a toothless smile. 'That the first durned sensible thing you have said in nearly three days!' He turned away as Prince, Wilson Cameron's old sheepdog, started barking. 'Lookee here! You see who's comin'?'

Luke Bragg turned and looked. Lena Flynn was coming towards them, slowly wading her filly through a sea of woolly sheep.

Tramp then said, 'It's Miss Lena!'

Bragg said nothing as he grinned at the old timer. He was thinking how fine she looked, how beautiful in the morning sun, a bright scarf about her head, scarlet mittens on her hands. Her horse moved slowly and the sheep scattered before her in their stupid way, protesting, pattering over the iron-hard ground. The woman came towards him through a pearly, almost unreal light, for the sky was heavy with snow, and yet still it did not come. The first snow of winter, and all about the great hills waited for it, the frozen streams waited, and the drooping jack pines. The air was as sharp as a Bowie knife's blade edge, and the bleating sheep blew clouds of mist into the air. From somewhere down the range there came the friendly sound of a barking dog, sharp and staccato.

Still she came on, not smiling, but watching him intently, as if she was ready to watch him for the rest of her days.

Then, without turning, Luke Bragg said, loud enough for the old timer to hear, 'Better get that coffee started, Rufus. And make sure there is enough for three.'

Tramp snickered and muttered, 'Of course I will make

enough for three, I ain't stupid ... I can count ... to at least three. ...' He smiled as he went to work on making the coffee.